THE LOVE OF LIFE & DEATH

by

KAE GALLA

&

KRISTEN COLLINS

Design: No Sweat Graphics & Formatting
Editor: Susette at My Write Hand VA

Printed in the United States of America

Contents

PROLOGUE

Once upon a time, eternity was simply darkness but out of that darkness, life was born. Creation was bountiful for a time until humans became greedy and Kronos had to do the unthinkable. The humans brought death upon themselves as their punishment.

Thus, Death was created. Over the centuries, he went by many names, the most common being Hades or the Grim Reaper. It would vary in different cultures. Death would carry out his duties ferrying the souls of humans, animals, and even different paranormal creatures into the afterlife where they would spend eternity. The only rules bestowed upon him were simple; do not reveal yourself to the living and do not take a soul before its time. Simple, easy rules, but so were the ones given to the humans in the Garden of Eden.

Throughout the years, the same solitary life became heartbreaking for Death, his only interaction was with his subjects of the

Underworld, other gods and goddesses on occasion and the dead he ruled over. He watched time and time again as they were reunited with their loved ones but he had no one to love himself. He longed to know how it felt to love and be loved in turn.

One day he came upon a beautiful woman at a well fetching water long after the cool morning time had passed. *What a dangerous place to be alone in this time period.* Her essence glowed around her, reminding him of the beauty of life coming into the world. As she gathered water, she hummed a whimsical tune. It called to him as if her siren voice was speaking to his cold dead heart.

He watched as she took the water back to the village, dispersing it to others until she came to a small hut on the far end, just outside of the small town. Death fought internally as he watched her every movement, entranced by her selfless manner.

At that moment, he decided he must know her. No one needed to know, and as long as he continued to do what he was created for, no one would, and so he disguised himself. *Surely, no one would know? Right?* A plan began to form. First, he would watch her, learn about her so as not to scare her. Besides, what did Death know of talking to another soul? Most of the time, his interactions were consoling the dead souls and guiding them into their eternal resting place.

The next day, he went to the well and waited for her. She came in the warmth of the day when the sun was at its peak. Death paced back and forth, rethinking his idea about revealing himself to her. He would disguise himself so that he didn't scare her, as well as to avoid being caught breaking the rules.

Taking a deep breath, he stepped out of the inbetween and fully into the human realm.

His first step forward a twig broke and her head snapped up, alerted to his presence, "Who's there?" she called.

"Sorry, my lady. I did not mean to frighten you. I mean you no harm. May I have a drink?" he asked quietly.

She watched him cautiously as she scooped a small cup of water out of the bucket and handed it to him, "What would your name be, stranger?"

"Hades. What might yours be, my lady?"

"Persephone."

He sat easily on the edge of the well, "May I ask as to why you're alone at the well at such a dangerous time of day? Don't you know there are scoundrels running amuck, waiting for ladies to make themselves vulnerable?" he smiled.

Persephone laughed, "Why? Are you one of them?"

He chuckled, "I must be on my way. Thank you, dear Persephone, for fulfilling my thirst. Maybe I'll see you around again sometime…"

"Oh, the mysterious type; I'm intrigued now, good sir. I do hope to run into you again sometime too," she replied with a smile.

A glint of something shiny caught her eye on the edge of the well. It was a necklace made of silver with a flower caressing the crescent moon. Hades turned and left the way he came, slipping into the inbetween as Persephone ran after him.

"Hades! You forgot your necklace!" she yelled but was stumped when he was nowhere to be found.

Death smiled as he stood in front of her, his ghostly hand caressed her face as he leaned in and whispered, "That is for you."

Her eyes widened as she glanced around at the realization that Hades was not a normal human being. She ran her fingers over the metal, tracing the intricate crevices and shape of the flower wrapped around the moon.

He left her presence, feeling alive for the first time in his entire existence. What a silly thing to feel such desire and passion for someone you barely even know. Hades knew what he must do, he must have her to spend eternity with. As the god of death, she could live as his queen in the underworld with him.

For weeks, Hades returned to the well to see Persephone. They talked the afternoon away in the shade away from the prying eyes of the villagers. Until one day, Persephone wasn't at the well. In fact, she was nowhere to be found.

After slipping into the inbetween and searching the entire village, Hades circled back to the well to see Persephone's soul on her knees at the well, leaning on the ledge, crying softly in pain.

"Persephone?" he called heartbroken.

At her name, she turned back to see Hades in his true form, "Hades? Why do you look so...different?" Realization dawned on her as she fully took in the being that stood before her. "You are the god of death!"

Tears fell down Hades cold cheeks, "I don't understand. How? Why?"

Her eyes wandered downward to the depths of the well saddened.

Persephone came to Hades and took his hands into hers, "It does not matter, my love. What matters is that I will be with you in the afterlife now."

Kronos, the creator of all creation appeared before them, brilliant in his aura surrounding him. "Hades, you have broken our sacred rules. It pains me to punish you but I cannot allow the transgressions that have passed to go on."

Kronos lifted a hand towards Persephone but Hades stepped in front of her, blocking his path.

"Please, do whatever you must to me but do not harm her soul. She is the light of my existence and I cannot bear for her to be punished for what I have done. I have been a faithful servant all of my life, surely that must count for something, Father," Hades pleaded.

Taking a step back from the two lovers, he paced about for a moment before facing them again, "For breaking the sacred rules, I will not remove Persephone from this universe. Your love is great but you shall never be as one, only as two halves. Persephone will be the embodiment of life personified as you continue your days out ferrying and overlooking souls in the Underworld. Always just a breath away from one another. This shall be your punishment." As Hades begins to protest, Kronos raises his hand, silencing him. "I'm not finished, my son. You have done your job well for many eons. For that I wish to grant mercy. On the Autumn solstice, the two of you will be allowed to be with one another, but only until the night of the Spring solstice. Heed my words, Persephone must carry out her duties bringing life to the natural world and you must continue to manage your responsibilities in the underworld as well." The threat of death due to noncompliance is left hanging unspoken on the air between the trio.

But that's not where the story ends...in fact that's where our real story begins. In Arcadia, South Carolina located deep in the heart of Spartanburg County, Greek mythology comes to life.

Arcadia was a mysterious place, full of mythical creatures living in it, such as nymphs or nature spirits, dryads or tree spirits, centaurs or half-human, half-horse warriors, and other non-human beings, including several gods and goddesses.

That's just a tip of the iceberg of Arcadia's origin. Every year on the season's solstice, all the mythological creatures, gods, goddesses and even demigods come out of the woodwork to mingle together.

But before we can understand the present, we must keep digging into the past.

Chapter 1

PERSEPHONE

I awoke, made anew. I was no longer human but now a goddess. As fields of flowers surrounded me, I looked into the eyes of nymphs. They were all around, staring back at me full of curiosity.

"Mistress, are you okay?" One of them asked with concern.

"Hush, Rose! Let the mistress gain her composure! It's not every day you are transformed into a goddess." The other nymph rolled her eyes.

"I know that, Lily!" they bickered back and forth before I held up my hand stopping them.

"Who are you two? My memory is a bit foggy but I remember what I think are the most important parts of it. Where is Hades?"

They looked at one another sadly, "I am Lily and this is Rose, we're your ladies. We will tend to your needs as well as aid you in your tasks. Not only are you now the goddess of life but that of fertility and spring. The god of death, Hades, was allowed to escort you here for safety before Kronos sent him off."

"Condemned to live only a breath from one another yet to only be as one during nature's rest. I guess I should be grateful for the time between solstices," I said bitterly.

In my previous life, I was treated as an outcast by those in my village. Hades never made me feel unwanted or less than. Being with him is the only time I felt whole. Now I would only be able to see my love for two of the four seasons. Half of my life to live in the Underworld and the other in the world that despised me during my human life. I was tasked with keeping them alive by blessing them with bountiful crops and children.

How do I bring such life into a world I feel so separate from?

Rose and Lily helped me to my feet, "Demeter awaits you, mistress."

"Who is Demeter?" I ask confused.

"She is your mother, she sculpted your new form from the clay of this earth before breathing life into you," Lily answered me.

They led me deep into an alcove of the forest as nymphs and other creatures looked on in curiosity. I could hear their hushed whispers. Not wanting to take my discomfort out on them, I smiled and waved meekly at each one. Younglings showered my path with flowers.

Rose leaned over and whispered, "It's not every day that a new goddess is brought to life. This is a time of celebration even in your heartache and pain."

I reached over and squeezed her hand, feeling comforted by my new friends in this strange new world laid before me. The path would seem rough at first but at least I would get to be with my love, if only for a short time. For my own sanity, I must focus on the positives of my situation.

As we came into the clearing, Demeter sat on a wooden throne, branches weaved unnaturally together to make her seat. Next to her was a slightly smaller seat, I walked forward and instinctively bowed in front of her. The party came to a standstill and the music and festivities ceased as Demeter looked upon my face.

"My Lady, you summoned me?"

Demeter stood and looked me over, "My dear, you are the breath of life, with beauty far superior to that of Aphrodite herself." She lowered her voice a bit and laughed, "But don't tell her that. She gets her knickers in a twist when her vanity is attacked in any form." I smiled as she embraced me, "Come, come, Daughter. You must take your place next to mine for all to see."

I looked out to all the creatures as they hooped and hollered in celebration and smiled as Rose handed me a horn of mead to drink and Lily gave me a fresh platter of fruits. Oh they tasted like nothing I had ever tried before in my past life!

"Do you like it, Daughter?" Demeter asked.

"Yes, their taste is indescribable."

I found myself over the next few hours clapping and feasting, a few nymphs pulled me from my throne and we danced around the fire, giggling uncontrollably.

As I sat and rested on my seat, there were gasps around me as once again all eyes fell on me. Confused, I looked around to see blooms of flowers, the likes of which have never been seen before, appear all around the grove.

Lily whispered, "My Lady..." and pointed at the chair and around us.

"Oh, Daughter..." Demeter voiced in awe.

"What are they?" I mumbled, examining the newly floral throne I sat on.

Demeter looked them over, "These are new species. Therefore, you get to name them."

"But how? I don't understand." Confusion sounded in my voice.

She cupped my face in her hands as she spoke to me, "You are life personified and the goddess of spring. You bring and give life to all creations, including plants. Your powers are connected to your emotions. In time, you will learn how to control them all but tonight, we celebrate your rebirth."

"What of Hades? I am meant to spend the colder solstices with him in the Underworld."

"My dear...has no one told you?" Demeter asked.

"Told me what?" I asked, confused again.

"You two are to be wed on the eve of the Autumn solstice. Kronos decreed it himself, unless you do not wish that. We can protect you here and come up..."

I placed a hand on top of hers, causing her to pause, "No! I still wish to be with him." Looking away with a sad smile I said, "I just imagined it to be under different circumstances is all."

Demeter giggled and nodded her head knowingly, "As a god, much less a goddess, things rarely ever go as we hope, my Daughter. Sadly, this is a fact. Even as a human, a woman at that, you surely had hardships based on your gender alone."

"Well, yes but I thought once I became a goddess that things would be..." I trailed off but Demeter finished.

"Different?" Again she nodded, "Unfortunately not but we can avenge ourselves to an extent. So that is worth more than before, right?"

"Yes, indeed."

*****

In the months that followed, every day was a learning experience. Demeter worked with me patiently as I diligently learned to hone my craft to the best of my ability. Some days were harder than others but in my free time, I worked on my secret projects, gifts for my love in the Underworld.

I would task Hermes to send my little creations to him. We may not be able to be together until our solstice comes, but I don't intend to let him think I've forgotten or forsaken him.

Under the cloud of darkness, with the blackened sands in Santorini from the hidden city of Thera, a strange tune plagued my head until I couldn't resist it hitting my tongue like a siren wielding her voice.

I molded the black sand under the blood red harvest moon until a three-headed dog took form. Examining the pup, I placed a kiss on his forehead gently blowing air into his snout, thus blessing him with life. The sand dissipated leaving the live puppy before me.

Sniffing my hand, taking in my scent he flopped onto the grassy ground belly up waiting for a tummy rub. Giggling, I obliged his needs as all three tongues lolled out of their mouths.

"Oh, I really did create a little beast of chaos with you, didn't I, boy?" Their barks were the only answer of confirmation I needed. "You are to protect my love and the Underworld. You, Cerberus, are a special gift from me to him."

Lily stepped forward out of the shadows, "Should I summon Hermes for you, my Lady?"

"Yes. Can you make sure Cerberus is well on his way to the Underworld? And for the last time, can you call me Persephone? I had the nickname Kore in my human life too. Either will do, Lily," I asked politely.

"Anything for you...Kore," she said shyly before taking Cerberus away.

I continued practicing my skills when the hairs on my arms stood up uneasily. It felt as if I was no longer alone but whoever was near, was no friend of mine.

"I know you're there...whoever you are," I said out loud, annoyed. My words remind me of the day I met Hades, causing my heart to ache with longing once more.

A tall man, hidden in the shadows of the trees, appeared in the dim moonlight. His long blonde hair and smirk across his face immediately gave away who he was.

Zeus.

"A fine night to stare at the stars, is it not?" he said seductively.

"What can I do for you, Zeus?" The annoyance in my voice is evident.

"Such disrespect for the king of gods?" he challenged.

"The only king I serve is Hades, and you are not him," I rebutted.

"I could be, if that is what you desire," he coaxed.

A snort of laughter escaped me, "Forgive me but does that line actually work for you?"

He scoffed offended, "My brother seems to have bewitched you. Why else would my charm not affect you so?" His facade breaking.

"No bewitching, simply true love. Something you know nothing of. You must possess things rather than be equals with them for fear of them taking power over you. Maybe if you opened your eyes, you could see that Hera could be your greatest asset instead of a hindrance. Especially if you quit lying with every woman, goddess and human alike," I shot back.

His reputation is no secret, even as a new goddess, I've heard of his...exploits. I have no intention of ever allowing myself to be one of them.

There is nothing he can offer that would even hold a candle to my Hades.

Zeus cornered me enraged, "I could have my way with you if I so desired." He leans in as if to touch me. I try not to cringe, but the mere thought of him touching me is revolting. "I should take you here and now, just to teach you a lesson." He practically growls when he sees my expression.

"You have no right. You are on hallowed ground, and no god dares to disrespect hallowed ground." Silently, I thank my mother for ensuring our safety with such sacred lands. "Why did you come here? Are you that threatened by your brother's happiness that you have to try to steal it away? Or maybe it is fear that your older brother would show you the true strength of his power? I will be wed to Hades come Autumn solstice and you will not touch what is his."

I push against his chest, sending him backwards quite a ways. Roots burst up between us, forming a barrier so that he could not approach again. He looked in disbelief that a new goddess could possess such strength. To me though, it felt invigorating to not be afraid of any man, human or god alike.

"This is not over yet, goddess," he warned before disappearing into the night.

I sank to the grassy floor allowing all my fear and anxiety to escape and for the first time in my new life, I wept. Vines and plants of all kinds wrap me in a protective cocoon of sorts as I allowed myself this moment of weakness.

HADES

"If I had known that a woman in your life was what I needed to be able to make changes to the Underworld, I would have started setting up suitors centuries ago," Hecate said giddily.

My eyes rolled as I glanced over at Hecate. She was like an annoying little sister but has been my right hand since becoming the king of the Underworld.

"Yes, yes, yes...so you have told me on multiple occasions now. Look it has to be perfect and somewhat of a resemblance of the human realm. I want her to feel at home when she arrives on the Autumn Solstice," I stressed to Hecate.

She waved me off, "I cannot wait to meet your bride. We have much to discuss but you go about ferrying souls from the human realm as I redecorate down here!”

I turned around to say one more thing but her facade slipped and showed her true form. Hecate rarely showed others, but like my dear Cerberus, she has three heads. She tends to let the other two show when she is deep in thought, she says they help her think faster.

“Looks like you have plenty of umm…help.” I gestured to her up and down as she paid me no attention, “I’ll just check in on you all later.”

As excited as I am for the upcoming solstice, I can’t help but feel as if something isn’t quite right. Maybe I’m just being paranoid, but maybe there is something to this intuition thing. With so much to do, I do my best to ignore the unease and write it off as nerves.

PERSEPHONE

Temple duty had become a regular routine, where the townsfolk would come before Demeter and I, presenting gifts and offerings. It felt unnecessary, I even voiced this to Demeter once but she brushed it off saying, “If they don’t respect you then you will wilt and wither away in power.”

It tends to be a whole day full of feasts and music usually with no problems. We were nearing the end of the line of people coming with requests when a farmer walked up. Immediately, I could tell by his composure he felt himself above women and the act of bowing to one seemed to make his skin crawl.

"For such powerful goddesses, your lack of favor shone on us with crops only suited for that of the lowest sow is deplorable," he spat.

"What offering do you bring us?" Demeter asked with a raised eyebrow.

He laughed in disbelief, "Why would I bring two women of fake power anything after seeing how we have been treated? You are not worthy of worship and praise. I will go to Zeus' temple and tell of your lack of respect to us. He will not stand for it."

Rage began to build within me at the disrespect of the farmers that spoke curses rather than praise. I can't explain it, but I also can't ignore it. Flashes of knowledge formed in my mind. The men who worked the land in question were lazy and took for granted the gifts my mother and I have provided. They believed we should cultivate their lands and provide everything so that they could sit around and drink wine while bedding women. Darkness consumed me from the inside out as I stepped forward to address him.

"I am not worthy, you say?" I scoffed.

How dare he! This lazy, entitled man knows nothing about me. His words act as a catalyst to something I can't quite understand. The Persephone I've worked so hard to become was no longer in control but merely watching from within.

"We know nothing of you other than Kronos has punished you for an affair. Probably with Zeus, since women have been so easily swayed by him, it seems."

Demeter growled indignantly behind me on her throne inside the temple.

White hot rage courses through my veins at the mention of Zeus. He may bed any willing female he can find but I most definitely am *not* among his headcount, nor will I ever be. My hands clenched into fists and I can feel my nails cutting into my palms as I try to remain calm. My body turns cold, and it's as if I'm pushed to the back of my own mind as another part of myself steps to the forefront.

"Since you have decided to disrespect this temple, I think you may need some time to ponder over your poor choice of words," I hear myself say.

"Persephone, no!" Demeter warned but it was too late.

Clouds began to fuse in the sky, blanketing the land in darkness as I strode past him. Kneeling down, once outside, I laid my hand onto the soil taking the soul from the richness of the life that it possessed.

Turning back to the farmer, my voice dropped a few octaves, "Zeus has no power here and will not hear your plea. Do not come back until you have offerings to quench my thirst for wrath."

Instead of life, everything started to die and crumple across the land around us. People immediately started panicking at the sight of me as I stood up and squared my shoulders, red eyes revealing the darkness that lived deep within my soul.

Demeter held her composure as the 'guests' fled the temple. Once they were gone, her sternness was evident with me.

"Daughter, do you know what you have done?"

As if awaking from a bad dream, I felt horrified at my actions. "I couldn't control it. It was like someone else took over my body," I confessed as I rubbed my arms, trying to dispel the unnatural cold I felt.

But I couldn't tell her, I couldn't confess that I didn't fight the reaction either. That disgraceful man triggered feelings from the threats Zeus has made. I couldn't tell her that. If I did, then I'd have to tell her about the threats in the first place. She would be hurt that I didn't come to her with my pain, but I don't want to start any drama.

"I'm sorry, Mother. I lost control. Forgive me," I pleaded, as tears ran down my face.

She took me into her arms, "It is all right, Daughter, but we must make it right."

I nodded my head, "But he can suffer, right?"

Demeter laughed, "Yes, his disrespect will not go unpunished."

DEMETER

My daughter is an absolute delight. Every part of her radiates life and happiness. Despite the circumstances of her arrival in my life, I've never seen her allow sorrow or anger to take over her. Not like today.

When her eyes began glowing red, I knew something was wrong.

In front of the humans, I was forced to remain calm. I could not let on that this was an unplanned and unexpected reaction from my daughter, but deep down I was worried for her. No goddess should allow such a drastically unexpected emotion to take over, and if it truly was something she could not control...then we have bigger problems. The potential for destruction lies within her, that much is evident.

"At your service, my Lady," Hermes says cheerily as he meets me in the meadow after I summoned him.

"Hermes, finally. I have a special request. A...uh, secret request." Looking him in the eye, I do my best to express just how important this is.

"Of course. What can I do for you?" he says curiously.

"I need you to deliver this invitation." I hand him the sealed envelope with a name neatly written on the front.

He studies it before his brows furrow. "Lytta! What do you want to invite her here for?" His concern is evident, but I brush it off.

"There are some things I need to discuss with her," I state simply.

"What in all the worlds could you ever want to discuss with the goddess of rage?"

"Hermes, you know I love you, right?" I wait for his nod of acknowledgment before continuing. "I need you to trust me on this one. Unquestioningly."

He stands in front of me, shocked for several long minutes before swallowing hard. "Yes, of course."

As he walks away with the envelope in hand, I can't help but be thankful for his loyalty and his friendship with my daughter.

"Thank you, Hermes," I call out before he is out of sight.

I don't know what answers Lytta will be able to provide, if any, but I have to try. Lytta is the goddess of rage and fury. She is known to act irrationally and crazed. When she was young, she said she couldn't control it, but as she grew into her power she embraced the full force of her fury. Now, a mere whisper can send nations to war. If she can provide any insight at all, then it will be worth the risk of inviting such a volatile goddess onto my lands.

And if not?

We will cross that bridge if we must.

PERSEPHONE

The leaves were turning beautiful hues of red, yellow, and orange with the cooling of the weather. Which could only mean one thing.

The Autumn Solstice.

With the solstice approaching, it meant the wedding was fast approaching. What if Hades changed his mind?

"What makes you so quiet, Daughter?" Demeter asks as she sits on the cool grass next to me.

"Do you think he still wants me?" I say, voicing my fear.

"Oh, Sweetheart, of course he does. Why all this doubt?"

"When I was a human, I wasn't well...wanted. Hades was the only one who cared for me. After spending this time as a goddess, I've seen that there is so much more that exists than I ever could have imagined. I worry that I don't measure up to the other goddesses. Maybe he will regret being stuck with me."

"Now you stop right there. Do not question your worth, my beautiful Daughter. I'm so sorry that you were not treated well in your past life but I can assure you that Hades is just as head over heels in love with you now as he was when you were human."

It's hard for me to believe her, but I do hope she is right.

"In fact...wait right here," she says cryptically before walking to the tree line at the base of the hill we were sitting on.

HECATE

A tingling at the back of my skull draws my attention away from wedding plans. Someone outside of the underworld is summoning me. When it becomes insistent, I have no choice but to respond to the summons. I don't leave the underworld often. Most of us don't. On the few occasions that I have returned to the human world,

I've either gotten a gnarly sunburn, or been eaten alive by nasty bugs...Nope, that world is *not* for me.

"Ugh!" I groan as I prepare to leave the comfort of my underworld home.

Following the pull, I find myself standing in a lush forest. To my left is a meadow with a grassy hill.

"There you are," A familiar cheery voice says.

Rolling my eyes, I turn to Demeter. She's so annoyingly happy, it grinds my gears. "What do you want?" I ask.

"You know it wouldn't kill you to smile once in a while," she chastises.

"I smile when I have reason to. Coming to the human world does not count as a reason to smile."

Grabbing my hand, Demeter begins walking toward the hill, "Come on, there is someone I'd like you to meet."

"Huh? I don't have time for this, Demeter."

"Persephone, honey, there is someone I'd like you to meet," Demeter calls as we approach a slender form laying on the hillside gazing up at the clouds.

Persephone? My eyes widen as I take in the beauty before me. Her long hair flowing in the wind, her eyes alight with life, her aura pure of heart.

Falling to my knees before her, I bow my head in respect. "My Queen." The words leave my lips on a whisper of reverence. It's no wonder Hades fell in love with her. She radiates peace and love. There is an undertone of danger within her, but she covers it well, and I can sense that her pure heart would not allow her to be callous or evil.

"Queen?" I hear her question.

Looking up into her uncertain gaze, I can't believe she doesn't understand her place. "Yes, my Queen. I've been waiting to meet you for some time now."

Tilting her head to the side, I can tell she hasn't been informed.

"This is Hecate. She is your Hades' right-hand man and most trusted subject."

"More like his annoying little sister if you ask Hades," I smile.

At the mention of Hades, Persephone's eyes light up. Rushing forward, she bombards me with questions. "How is he? Has he been getting my gifts? Does he miss me? Does he still want to marry me?"

"Whoa, whoa, whoa, hold on there. Slow down," I laugh. "Yes, he has been getting your gifts and loves them all dearly. He is so excited to see you again, and what kind of question is that? Of course, he still wants to marry you!"

Her smile is so big, I worry the poor girl's cheeks will split.

"See, I told you," Demeter tells Persephone.

"You doubted him?" I ask, concerned.

"Our dear Persephone is doubting her worth," Demeter corrects.

"As we speak, Hades is going through every last wedding detail with a fine-toothed comb. He demands perfection, for his queen. The tower has been transformed into a beautiful venue filled with flowers and vibrant colors. You are the reason Hades gets up each day, you are his heart. Never doubt that." I know she won't understand the depth of his feelings for her until she is there with him, but I hope to at least relieve some of her fears.

We talk for the remainder of the evening, until I have no choice but to return to the underworld to perform my duties.

Persephone takes a handful of dirt in her hands. There is a soft glow emanating from within her clasped hands. As she slowly opens them, a small but bright blue flower emerges.

"Will you give him this for me?" she asks with a soft smile.

"Of course, but what is it?" I ask as I study the small petals.

"It's a Forget-me-not"

"I assure you, my Queen, he has never and will never forget you."

"Thank you, Hecate." She hugs me tight, before I take my leave.

Returning to the underworld is a rush. My senses are heightened here. It's as if my body protests being anywhere else.

As I approach Hades' office, I become nervous. *Will he be upset that I met her?*

"Enter," he says when I knock.

Slowly, I open the door, trying to judge his mood. If he is in an argument with one of his brothers, I'll need to diffuse the situation before I mention his bride. But he seems content as he reviews paperwork.

Looking up he sees me standing in the doorway, "Since when do you knock?"

"Um, I have something for you," I say, stepping closer.

Glancing around the room, I see his decanter and crystal glass set in the corner. Knowing it won't be used tonight, I grab one of the glasses and place the roots of the new plant inside, before handing Hades the glass itself.

His spine straightens as he sees what I've brought. "Hecate?"

"Please don't be mad," I caution.

"That all depends on the next words to come out of your mouth."

"Persephone was having wedding jitters and worried that she wasn't good enough for you, so Demeter summoned me to alleviate her fears."

"She's having second thoughts?" he asks, concern written all over his face.

"NO! No, she's not. She was worried that *you* were having second thoughts, and that she was trapping you. That girl has a heart of pure gold, you know."

"I'd never have second thoughts where she is concerned."

"I told her that. She made that for you," I say pointing at the plant. "She said it's called a Forget-me-not."

He smiles as he inspects the tiny flower.

"I'm glad I got to meet her, but I'm sad that it couldn't have been you to see her," I say honestly.

"Thank you, Hecate. Thank you for easing her mind and bringing me this gift."

With a slow nod, I turn and leave Hades to enjoy his gift in peace.

Chapter 2

ZEUS

Hera has been in that damned closet all day. It's bad enough that her closet is almost as big as our master suite, but does she really need to use my closet for shoes? I've been relegated to a small section, but it's only a matter of time before I have to start using one of the closets in the guest rooms. Seriously, the woman has a serious fashion problem.

"I have things to do, woman! What, in Kronos name, are you even looking for?"

She peeks her head out, "You can't seriously expect me to just grab a dress out of here on the day of the wedding. I have to plan it out and make sure it is perfect." Rolling her eyes at me, she disappears back into the depths of her clothes.

"This is about that stupid wedding?" I can't believe she's making such a big deal out of this.

"It's not some random wedding of a lesser god and goddess. This is your brother we are talking about here. He's family, which means she will be family. I want to make a good impression when we meet her, and I can't do that in rags," Hera says dramatically.

"Hera, honestly love, I'm sure she isn't *that* impressive."

"Don't be silly, Zeus. Have you heard what the nymphs have said about her? She has made quite the stir already and she is only in her infancy."

"Quite the stir," I laugh humorlessly. "She is all I hear about all day long. I mean come on, she is just a human who had the misfortune of getting on my father's bad side. It's not like she's this great beauty or anything. As far as we know, she's just a gold-digging cow. She probably has a distasteful ego, and after being reborn as a goddess, she most likely thinks everyone else is beneath her. I mean seriously, who does she think she is?"

Peeking her head out a second time, "I should just go to the shops and get something new. Do you think it's too late for a custom garment?"

When I just look at her like she's lost her mind, she shrugs before disappearing once again.

Has all of Olympus fallen under Persephone's spell? I don't get it, I really don't. Sure she is beautiful, and her heart appears pure, but what fun could such innocence be? There is a spark in her eyes, unlike that of the other goddesses, she has a vibrance and love for life that is invigorating. Sadly though, she has poor judgment and has refused my every advance. I've given her multiple chances in these months to change her mind but she is stubborn.

What I wouldn't give to claim that innocence, and tame the spark within. Why should Hades get to have her? He broke the rules after all. Besides, what does he have to offer that I don't? Hades hasn't even been with a woman in eons. She should be with a god who can show her how a man-

"Well, are you going to just stand there or are you going to come with me to the shops? I'd like your input," Hera says, interrupting my thoughts.

HADES

There was a time when eternity seemed dull and meaningless. My father, Kronos, was not the paternal figure anyone would hope for, not in a million millennia. When my brothers and I were formed, there was no celebration of cigars and "man hugs" with his nearest and dearest. Instead, Kronos held contempt for our mere existence. *Odd, considering the amount of work we do for him.*

We may be kings in our own rights, but make no mistake, our father did not allow us to take our thrones easily. As the years went on, and Kronos realized he was stuck with his trio of sons, he took special interest in our abilities. Some say my father had lost his mind by the time my brothers and I came of age and giving so much power to each of us was his way of relieving himself of his own responsibilities. Others believe it to be a calculated move...to what ends no one is certain.

As for me? I'm just glad he leaves me alone for the most part. My brothers have their freedom, while I was cursed to a life without, well just that, *life*. Every aspect of my day, my job, my existence, involves death. No matter where I turn, no matter what I do, I am surrounded by it.

And make no mistake, for the bringer of death, there is no vacation time.

Each day, I see the living going about their lives, giving no thought to my purpose, not until they are near the end. Close enough to witness so much joy and love, but never to touch. As wars and illness raged, my job became torture. *Don't these mortals know how much potential they have?*

So many blessings, so many opportunities to achieve greatness and yet they chose hatred, greed, and death. Their souls pay the price for the deeds of their mortal experiences. Meanwhile, Zeus plays with his lightning as he beds goddess after goddess behind his wife's back and Poseidon parties like an adolescent beneath the seas. Neither knows the burden I carry with me each and every day.

The constant and endless routine became mind numbingly dull.

I was desperate for companionship.

Not the sort of companionship that comes from someone under my rule. Not the sort of companionship that comes from those who frolic about as if their actions mean little in the grander scheme of things...Not the sort of companionship of the gods.

I craved life. To feel the warm touch of someone who knew the value of their existence. Someone who knew time was important, but even more so the way you treat others matters.

By now, everyone in Olympus knows our story. Many have asked why I would risk such a thing. Why would I show myself to a human, knowing the consequences? Several goddesses have expressed their disgust and disappointment at not being approached before -what they considered- a lowly human, but that just proved why I could never have been with one of them. They are vapid and vain and have no values to speak of. They are the opposite of my Persephone.

From the first time I saw her at that well, I knew she was the one. Her essence was so pure and her aura glowed with integrity. I watched her selflessly share what little she had with those less fortunate in her village, and never ask for anything in return. She never let the negativity of the world get to her.

How could I not approach her? How could I not try to speak to such a lovely rarity in this world of destruction and hatred?

I cherish the time we had together, but I also look forward to our future. Despite being separated for half of the year every year, I cannot regret the decisions I've made that brought us to this point.

Now if only the Autumn solstice could get here so I can hold my love in my arms once more.

Her gifts have been wonderful, but we have not been permitted to see one another or communicate any other way. I wish I could be there with her now. The shift her life has taken as she has embraced her new goddess powers must have been difficult. I have to trust that Demeter is taking care of her and preparing her for her time in the underworld, because once we are married she will rule at my side during her portion of the year here. If she doesn't want to act as a queen she doesn't have to, but I want her to know how important she is to me and that means including her in every part of my existence. Even if she is only queen in name, she will be afforded all the respect that comes with the title.

The underworld is aflutter with excitement as preparations for our wedding are made. Everyone is excited for the changes that have already begun. With each of Persephone's gifts, the underworld has become a brighter place. Plants and flowers bloom in the darkness, some emitting their own illumination. The general feeling among my people is joyful and that positivity is spreading.

As I think of our upcoming nuptials, I want everything to be perfect for her.

Hecate wants to task Cerberus, the three-headed dog Persephone created for me, as bearer of the rings. I don't see how that will work. He's a good boy, don't get me wrong, but the pup is a ball of energy that leaves a trail of slimy slobber wherever he goes. Cerberus is a great companion and his training as a guard dog is coming along well, but he is still just a pup with a short attention span. I can't imagine casually and calmly walking down a wedding aisle with two delicate rings tied around his necks would be his idea of a good time.

But Hecate tells me to "trust her vision," so that is what I'm going to do. Even I have to admit, the bowtie collars she got him are adorable and I can imagine the smile on Persephone's face when she sees him, *IF* he can behave.

Almost everything is ready for my bride's arrival. Almost. A groom should have a gift for his bride. It's a detail I've thought long and hard over.

Material things aren't the way to show someone you love them, but there is something I can give her that I think she will appreciate.

While planning the ceremony, Hecate mentioned that Demeter asked her to be in charge of the bridal bouquet. This is something I can do for my bride. I can make her a one of a kind bouquet that will outshine any other.

As I sit on the floor in the darkness of my bedroom, I rub my hands together slowly, over and over. My palms warm with the movement.

My bride isn't like others. She would hate to see a flower's life cut short simply for the benefit of a visual display. Which is why all floral decorations for the ceremony are live plants, either in pots or planted strategically for the occasion. This wasn't hard to accomplish since our ceremony will take place in the new gardens just outside the tower's perimeter.

The heat between my hands intensifies as the image in my mind becomes clearer.

My bride isn't like others. She would prefer simple beauty over extravagance. She values life and love above all else. One of my many abilities is to create precious gems, the likes of which humans covet. But that doesn't faze Persephone. She loves me for me, even before she knew about my abilities.

Opening my hands, I can see a soft blue glow emanating from the space between them. The glow comes from a single large rose. The rose is a solid diamond, formed out of my love for her. A single rose may not be a traditional bouquet, but it is a symbol of our love that she will be able to take with her always. Even when we are apart, she will be able to look at it and know that I am always in her heart.

Every part of me aches to see her. To hold her in my arms and breathe in her fresh floral scent. I can't imagine how she is feeling, I just hope she is as excited as I am, without the nerves. It would be so easy for her to choose an easier life, in the human world or on Olympus with the others.

Stop! I scolded myself. I cannot doubt our love, not ever.

Now to make sure everything goes off without a hitch at the wedding, and of course keep my brothers away from her.

PERSEPHONE

I felt like an Autumn Solstice wedding was a great comparison of the relationship Hades and I shared. Everything on earth was starting to go into hibernation for the colder winter months. Plants were wilting and dying but in Spring, when I returned to the mortal realm, they would be reawakened and revived.

For our wedding, Hades was opening the gates of the underworld for the gods, goddesses, and creatures of Olympus and the mortal realm to attend. My mother, Demeter, and I walked through the portal through the Gate of Dawn that led to the dock and the ferryman that is one of the few entrances to the underworld.

Lily and Rose in tow, guiding the Arcadian horses that were pulling wagons of my things since this would be my first visit to the underworld. Jitters ran through every part of my body.

"Kore, you have to stop fidgeting. You're going to drive everyone crazy before the wedding begins and we're already overwhelmed with details of your nuptials," my mother chastised.

Water lilies floating on top of the glassy surface as we stepped aboard the ferryman's raft. Transparent glows of fireflies illuminated sporadically around us making me giggle. As a human, I always wondered where animals and bugs would go after death or if they would cease to exist.

I felt comfort that I would be able to always be with them and not just humans. Demeter gently touched my shoulder, pulling me from my own thoughts.

"Kore, we have arrived." Looking past me, her smile widened a bit more. "And so have the guests, it seems."

Peering behind me, over my shoulder, I saw gods and goddesses dressed in grand clothing made of silks and the finest linens floating towards us. The raft smoothly docked on the shores of the underworld that led to Hades' palace grounds.

"The underworld is much more beautiful than the tales I've heard," I noted to my mother.

Lily and Rose exchanged a look that Demeter noticed as she answered, "Well, Hades has you and the guests coming through the side of the realm that is considered in the human world as heaven. If we had entered through the Gate of Dusk then we would have passed all the damned and tormented souls." She placed a comforting hand on top of mine as she reassured me. "He didn't want to frighten you on your first time in the underworld."

I nodded, "I guess there will always be good and bad no matter what realm you reside within."

The next moment Lily and Rose were whisking me away towards the entrance of the stone castle, Hecate was pacing back and forth in her true form, barking orders from each of her mouths.

"Cerberus, no!" someone shouted.

Then I felt it before I saw it. In an instant, I was on the ground as slobbering tongues attacked my face from every angle. Uncontrollable laughter overtook me as I caressed my creation with love. He had grown significantly since I sent him off down here but he was everything I had hoped to bring to Hades in my absence.

"So, I guess this means you remember me?" His responding barks answered my question.

"My Queen!" An underworld nymph pulled Cerberus off of me, quivering apologetically, "My Lady! My apologies! I should have held onto him tighter! Please forgive me."

"Titus! As Cerberus' trainer, your one and only job is to train and control him!" Hecate screeched embarrassed.

"Yes, my Lady," he answered.

My heart felt saddened at his fear, "It is all right. It is not his fault, Hecate. I'll handle this." She stepped aside waiting as Titus cowered before me.

Instead, I looked over at Cerberus, whistling and snapping my fingers in command, "Cerberus, sit." Immediately, he obeyed. I cupped his heads in my hands looking into his eyes to gain his focus, "You will obey those who are in charge. You may be born of chaos but you will only inflict it when allowed. Is that clear?"

At that, his answering response was rolling over belly up in submission as Hecate laughed, "I'll be damned."

"Aren't we all?" I joked which made everyone burst out in laughter.

The next few hours passed in a blur as Lily and Rose went to work preparing me for the wedding. I had not seen Hades since arriving. Apparently gods were just as superstitious as humans about not seeing their significant other before the bride walks down the aisle.

I hadn't realized that I had dozed off when Lily gently shook my shoulder, awakening me, "My Lady," she whispered, "It's time."

She and Rose helped me to my feet as they lifted the dress over my shoulders. Silky and material white as ivory draped over my body in all the right places. A gold ring pinched the fabric on top of my left shoulder and another around my waist.

Examining myself in the mirror, I could hardly recognize myself anymore. I was not the human I once was a short time ago. Demeter walked up, looking me up and down with pride.

"I feel like you're being stolen from me when I finally have you. You look so beautiful, Daughter. Hades is a very lucky man but if he hurts you then I will tear the underworld apart to avenge you."

I nod in understanding but smile knowing that her threat is unnecessary.

"The wedding dress is borrowed, it was mine once upon a time." She looked away and I could feel her sadness before she wiped away a tear from her eye and continued, "But that is a story for another time. The crown is something new, as the queen of the underworld."

"Your necklace is something old," Lily smiles, referring to the necklace Hades had left on the edge of the well the day we met.

Touching the precious gift that I have never taken off. As my emotions start to build, Forget-Me-Nots adorn my hair and gown adding an aspect of my personality to it.

Rose pulled my foot up and slipped my shoe from my foot, dropping a drachma coin into the toe, "This is just an old wives' tale of luck from Lily and I, my Lady."

Demeter turned toward Hecate, opening a box and pulling a blue diamond rose from the case. "And something blue from Hades to you."

"He was worried you would be displeased if your bouquet was made of real cut flowers. He said you wouldn't want to see their lives cut short, so he crafted this especially for you, my Queen," Hecate confessed.

"It is so beautiful. I will cherish it always," I whispered in awe as I examined every detail.

Hecate touched my arm, "Your Majesty, it's time."

I nodded quietly. Butterflies filling my belly threatened to take over but my feet were practically trying to fly me down the aisle to my Hades.

Stopping me from entering everyone's view, Hecate held me steady, "You wait here. When you hear the lyre start then you enter. It'll take a moment before it starts. Are you okay by yourself?"

"Thank you, Hecate. I'll be fine. It'll give me a moment to catch my breath before facing all...of them."

We both peeked around the corner briefly and she rolled her eyes at Aphrodite chastising Hephaestus' wardrobe choice while trying to maintain her composure. Her vanity was something in itself.

I laughed, waving her off, "Hecate, go before they start a riot in there. I can manage to walk on my cue. Wait for the lyre, see?"

Shaking her head, she walked off. Once I realized I was finally alone, I let out a breath I hadn't realized that I had been holding. I shook my hands out. The truth is I wanted to forget this whole ceremony thing and just take Hades right there at the end of the aisle but that would really send all of the underworld and Olympus into a gossip frenzy.

"If you're having second thoughts, I can forgive you of your past shenanigans and let bygones be bygones. I'll take you away from here. All you need to do is say yes."

Zeus reached out to touch me and I hissed, jerking away from his hand. The thought of feeling his hand on my skin made me want to vomit.

My shoulders slumped at the recognition of his voice, "How do you think Hades would feel if he knew his brother was responsible for my human death? And that when my death backfired and I was reborn, that same brother continued to pursue me?"

The anger in his eyes intensified at my threat, "First you mock me, now you threaten me? I see that brains were not a gift from your mother during your rebirth?" he spat.

I circled him, knowing I had him cornered this time, Hera's laugh was loud as she and Athena were becoming animated in their banter.

Pointing upward, "Aw, I see your wife isn't far away. Maybe all of Olympus and the Underworld should know that the king of gods would dare to challenge his brother not only in his home but on his wedding day."

"You wouldn't…"

"Oh but I would. You see, Zeus, I am not afraid of you and I quite literally have you by the balls. So you see I have learned something in my rebirth even though that time may still be short compared to yours. I am both life and death, I am the balance you have always feared." I stepped forward as his facade wavered, "Now that I am to be wed to Hades we will be the most powerful couple and if I so much as suspect you have been within a 20-foot radius of my husband and I after this day for any other reason than official business duties, I will destroy you and the kingdom you have built."

"No one would believe you so your threats are empty," he argued and I laughed.

"You cannot really be that ignorant nor naive of your reputation not just with humans but the gods. They would believe it and it would be a grave you would not be able to dig yourself out of ever." The lyre started to play and I exhaled a relieved breath upon hearing my cue, "You better find your seat, Zeus, before anyone suspects foul play."

I cut past him and made my way around the corner, my adrenaline was on fire in my veins but when my eyes fell upon Hades all of the bad, the pain, the suffering, and the doubts simply vanished.

I tried to suppress my laughter when my eyes fell upon Cerberus and the bow ties around each neck. Between his three heads he carried the rings that Hades and I would wear.

The aisle felt never ending as I tried not to run down the aisle to my soulmate, his mouth hung agape staring at me. Poseidon reached around and pushed his mouth closed as he swiped his hand away and the crowds chuckled.

"You look stunning, my Queen."

Reaching my hand out to take his, electricity ran between us and I felt a connection that was far superior to anything I felt for him as a human. Hades brought my hand to his lips, placing a gentle kiss as his lips brushed across my knuckles. We smiled and just stared at one another speechless. One of the Fates coughed to pull our attention away from one another.

"Oh. I'm sorry. What did you say?"

They looked at one another knowingly and smiled then continued in unison. With ribbons they bound our hands together.

"From this moment on, you Hades, god of the underworld and death, and you Persephone, goddess of life and spring, your destinies will always be intertwined. Bound are your souls and now your fates." They slipped rings onto our fingers, "These rings will be a symbol of your vows to one another."

Hades took me into his arms, laying me back as his lips fiercely interlocked with mine in front of every being present. The crowd erupted into cheers and applauded us as newlyweds. We held our bound hands high into the air for all to witness.

Zeus rolled his eyes as Hera watched him with her brows furrowed, I had a feeling today's little act of defiance would not be let go easily. How many times can I scorn the king of gods before he finds the ammunition he needs to take his revenge out on me?

I shook the thought from my head as we walked back down the aisle. We came two separate beings but will leave as one being bound for all eternity to one another. I was not about to let Zeus take that from me, not today.

Just out of eyesight, Hades pulled me to his chest as I wrapped my arms around his neck, letting him kiss me deeply. There was an animalistic craving building from within and I needed him. I wasn't sure how much longer I could wait to satiate my hunger.

The moment was broken as Zeus put his hands on both of our shoulders, "I hate to interrupt the two of you."

A growl escaped Hades as I tried to nonchalantly pull away from Zeus' touch. Hera stepped forward and embraced me. Something about it felt awkward but I ignored it.

"Ignore my husband. He doesn't know how to read a room. That is my skill," she said sarcastically, rolling her eyes at Zeus.

I leaned in and whispered, "Men rarely do," and winked which caused us both to giggle a bit.

"Anyway, we will leave you two be but we wanted to be the first to congratulate you both on your union. We will see you at the reception." Hera nodded at Hades before practically dragging her husband away by the arm. "Come, husband. I'm starving and I hear the mead made in the underworld is top notch."

Once out of sight, Hades put his hands on each side of my arms, "I'm sorry about my brother. He's not known for his tact."

I grasped his hands on me, "It's okay, my love."

"You looked really uncomfortable, almost in distress. He does that to women sometimes. Are you sure you're okay?" His face held so much concern for my well-being.

I plastered a smile across my face trying to lock away every bad feeling Zeus inspired into a pit in the back of my mind for another day. Today, at this moment, it was all about Hades and I. The moment we have been waiting for since my transformation into a goddess.

"Yes, my King. Let's not keep the guests waiting. The faster we get through this reception, the faster I get to have you all to myself finally." I winked, biting my lower lip.

Hades ran his thumb across my lips and leaned down, "Now who's a little scoundrel?" he chuckled and kissed me again.

"What can I say? You must be rubbing off on me or something," I laughed.

"There you two are!" Hecate chastised, "The guests are waiting! Even the king and queen of the underworld are forbidden from missing a good party! Especially one that I spent endless hours planning just for you two. Do you know how hard it was to coordinate an event that *all* of the gods and goddesses could attend at one time?" she ranted on but Hades and I only had eyes for each other.

She rolled her eyes as she pushed us towards the party. Hades winked at me, leaning down and whispering, "Soon you will be mine completely."

His promise sent chills down my spine, ecstasy awaited us both and so did our new adventure together.

LYTTA

Under normal circumstances, I wouldn't be caught dead at a social event such as a wedding, but this one is different and not just because it's a royal wedding.

I watched as all the gods and goddesses I loathe pretend to be something they are not. They all boast about how perfect and blessed their lives are, putting on a show as if the opinions of the pantheon actually matter. If only the truth were at the forefront. Now that's a party I'd buy tickets for. I'd kill to see them put in their place.

Not everyone here is bad, I wouldn't have come if that was the case. I watch as the newlywed couple make their rounds. Persephone radiates happiness and I can't help but want to be happy for her, even if my own heart is jaded.

"Persephone, this way. There is someone I'd like you to meet," Hades says as he guides her in my direction.

Her eyes light up when she sees me. Rushing toward me, my lips twitch and threaten to form a smile as I watch the shock form on Hades' face as he follows behind her.

"Oof," I grunt as Persephone collides into me, hugging me with all her might.

"Lytta! I'm so glad you came," she gushes.

"So, I guess you already know each other," Hades comments.

"Oh, yes. Lytta is a good friend," Persephone confirms happily.

Hades dramatically clutches his chest as he turns his attention to me. "Ouch, I'm hurt, Lytta. I thought I was your only friend," he says teasingly.

I roll my eyes, "Yeah, well I made another, my King."

"You live here?" Persephone asks excitedly.

Slowly, I nod, "Yeah, well, hell is the perfect place for someone like me to work, if you know what I mean," I wink.

Early on, Hades recognized my knack for punishment and torture, but rather than criticize or chastise me for it, he found a place for me. Somewhere that I can excel, thrive even. His lack of judgment made it easy for me to open up and be myself around him.

"I'm sorry to interrupt, I just wanted to congratulate the lovely couple," Proteus says, interrupting our little conversation.

Proteus is one of Hades' nephews. *Poseidon's son* I think to myself. He and his father never really saw eye to eye, so Hades became the father Proteus always wanted. They have a special bond to this day. From what Demeter has told me, of all of Hades' family, Proteus is her favorite.

Persephone hugs me again before they are whisked away into the crowd once more.

HADES

Persephone places her diamond rose carefully on the end table next to the bed, her smile never wavering. Silently, I close the door behind us and approach her from behind. I won't rush her, and I don't want her to feel pressured into doing anything she isn't ready for, but I crave closeness with her, even if it's a simple touch of the hand.

Wrapping my arms around her waist, I marvel in her warmth as she leans into me, her back pressed against my front. We bask in the calm surrounding us for a time before she breaks the silence.

"My mother tried to give me 'the talk' last night," she says matter of factly.

I can't help but tense at her calm statement. My desire for her is a live wire in my entire body. Clearing my throat, I ask, "Oh, and uh...how did that go?"

"Awkwardly," she giggles. "But it was sweet of her to make the effort, even if I already knew the mechanics of it."

"The mechanics and the real act are two very different things, my Queen."

"I know," she says as she turns her head to look at me. "I'm not afraid."

"Not even a little?" I tease.

Shaking her head she turns in my arms, reaching up to wrap her own around my neck. "Not even a little."

"That makes one of us," I admit.

Her eyes widened slightly at my admission.

"You see, my love, it has been a very long time for me. I worry that in my...enthusiasm, I could be too rough with you. I never want to hurt you, especially not in our bed."

"Oh, Hades, you could never hurt me," she reasons.

"But I did. It's my fault we have been cursed with our separation. I was selfish and you paid the price," I say, voicing my guilt.

"Because of you, I have been made anew. I am able to do things and be someone that I never imagined. I can make a difference. And as for that curse? It is also a blessing. Yes, we have to be apart for six months of the year, but we also get to be *together* for six whole months every year."

Resting my forehead on hers, I can't help but breathe a sigh of relief. Part of me worried that she blamed me for our situation. "How did I get so lucky to have you as my soul mate?"

"I'm the lucky one," she says.

"We will have to agree to disagree on that fact." Leaning forward, I press a gentle kiss to her lips.

"Hades," she breathes as she pulls back, "I love you and I want to be yours in *every* way."

With a smile and a confidence only true love can afford, I lean in for a deeper kiss. "As you wish, my Queen."

Garment by garment, our clothes find a new home on the bedroom floor. Their value of little importance, sentimental or otherwise. The only thing that mattered in that moment was binding ourselves to one another in every way possible. As our vows play through my mind, I can't get over the fact that this wonderful woman is my wife. From now until the end of time, we are one unit.

Looking at my beautiful bride, I'm met with perfection. Every inch of her is absolute perfection. Her porcelain skin is silky to the touch. Goosebumps rise to greet my fingertips as I caress each and every inch of her body.

I wish I had something better to offer her than my scar-riddled flesh. Just as the thought crosses my mind, Persephone traces each fine line with a finger, her eyes never leaving mine as she does. Most of my chest and back is covered in razor thin lines as evidence of my past. Some litter my thighs and rear as well.

"One day," she says softly, "I wish to hear about these."

Reflexively, I flinch away from her touch, and reach for the sheet to cover the marks.

"No. Do not hide yourself from me, Hades. You are beautiful. I only wish to know so that I can know you better." Persephone kisses the largest of my scars, the one that runs the full length of my chest, before kissing another and another.

I can't bear the reverence in her touch.

Pushing her to the bed, I capture her mouth with mine once more. My hand travels the length of her body before cupping her breast. As I tease the sensitive peak, her nipple hardens in response and she moans.

Abandoning her lips, I take her other nipple in my mouth, sucking and nipping harder and faster as her moans urge me on. There is no nervous tension in her body, so I trail one hand down the side of her ribcage, making a path across her flat stomach and down further to the most intimate place between her legs.

"Yes," she hisses.

With her encouragement, I caress her nub in slow circles, finding a rhythm that resonates with her. Her nails rake across my back as she tries to pull me closer to her. My tongue and finger work together to ease the passage within, readying her for me.

Slowly, I push one finger inside of her, allowing her body to show me what she is ready for. Persephone rocks her hips into my hand, and my finger slides in deeper.

"I-I need...I need..." she pants.

"What do you need, my love?" I stop to ask.

"You. I need you. I need you inside me," she says between breaths.

"Are you sure?" I can't help but ask the question.

"Yes!" she yells, before taking me by surprise as she pushes me onto my back and straddles my waist.

I'm so surprised by her actions that I don't have time to caution her or slow her down.

Persephone rocks her hips on top of me, rubbing her heated center over the hard length of my shaft. Leaning forward, I feel her silken touch as she positions me beneath her entrance. She lowers herself too quickly for someone with no experience.

A whimper escaped her lips as she stills above me. Her eyes shut tightly.

"Baby, are you okay?" I ask, knowing that breaking through her virginity must have been painful. I rub her arms and back comfortingly, at a loss for what else to do.

She nods, but her eyes remain closed.

"I'm going to need the words, my love," I say anxiously. I can feel her body trembling. As much as I want to move and connect our bodies the remainder of the way, I know she needs time to adjust to the intrusion.

"I...I just need a minute to adjust," she breaths.

"Let me help you." Reaching down, I find the place above where our bodies are joined and I slowly begin to rub circles around her clit once more.

Her head falls back and she gasps at the sensation. It doesn't take long for her hips to start moving in a tentative rocking motion. Slow and shallow at first, but with increasing urgency.

"That's it baby, just like that," I encourage.

Placing her hands on my chest, she stabilizes herself as she allows her hips more range of motion. Her gaze, hooded now, glistens with desire as she looks into my own eyes. She gasps as I slide further into her. Letting her set the pace is a new form of torture. My balls ache for release, but I refuse to let this end prematurely like some prepubescent loser.

Persephone tries to set a constant pace but her heightened desire has her rushing her movements. With a hand behind her head, I guide her lips to mine before flipping positions again. As she gazes up at me, I pull out slowly before entering her fully.

"More, please," she begs.

"Always," I respond before increasing my pace as I enter and retreat.

My hips flow in a fluid motion as I bring her to first one and then multiple orgasms, ensuring she is fully satisfied before I find my own release. I'll never get enough of this feeling. Persephone is everything to me, and feeling her wrapped around me, is the best feeling in all the worlds.

We make love through the night and late into the next morning.

Chapter 3

LILY

It is a blessing to be able to witness such pure and true love. Hades dotes on Persephone as if she is his only reason for breathing. When we are in the mortal realm, Persephone brings joy to those around her, but here with Hades? That joy is not just for others. She radiates it from within.

My heart swells as I watch their every interaction, hoping to one day find someone to love that much.

Lately, I've been noticing that our queen has been out of sorts. She's been sleeping in later and later. When food is served, dishes that used to appeal to her now turn her stomach. Rose was in her bedroom trying on a new perfume and Persephone was able to smell it from outside in the garden.

I have a feeling I know what's going on.

"Can I talk to you for a minute, my Lady?" I ask as I knock on the door of her bedroom after her afternoon nap.

"Of course," she says cheerfully.

"I'm not really sure where to start," I admit.

Tilting her head to the side, she appears concerned. "Whatever it is, you can tell me."

"I know, it's just that...I've been noticing some things."

"What kind of things?"

I take a deep breath, "Changes in you. I've been noticing some things that I believe mean something important." *Does she know already?* I don't want to take the joy of telling people away from her if she does, but if she doesn't then I feel like it's my responsibility to help her find out if my suspicions are correct.

"I'm sorry, I don't think I understand."

"I believe you are pregnant, my Lady."

Her jaw drops and her eyes widen at my words.

"Foods you normally love make you ill, your sense of smell has heightened, and you've been extra tired lately...Is it possible that you are with child?"

PERSEPHONE

Glancing out over the moors of Moirai, I looked up the staircase towards the Cave of Fates, where The Fates themselves reside. They would give me the answers I needed but my mind wandered back to Hades, always Hades.

His door was shut to his study which meant he was busy. Usually I wouldn't disturb him but this news could not wait.

My knuckle tap-tap-tapped against the wooden door.

"You don't have to knock, Kore. Your distraction is always welcome in our home," Hades chuckled.

"Hello, my love," I whispered, overcome with so many emotions at once.

Not only had I just discovered I was with child and according to the healers the child is quite a way into development, but I was about to have to leave my love for the most important part of it all...and he won't be there when our child is born.

As I slowly entered his study, he looked up from his desk. The furrow of my brows must have given way to my distress because he was out of his seat in an instant, concern written all over his features.

"Did something happen? Are you upset about having to leave?"

"No, well yes I am, but this is something we need to discuss and I just don't know how to tell you this with my departure right around the corner. I feel like I just arrived yesterday," I cried.

Hades lifted me into his arms and sat on the couch with me in his lap. My arms locked around his neck and I buried my face into his chest, breathing in his scent for comfort.

Taking deep breaths, the words just fell out of my mouth as he stroked my head, "I'm with child, Hades."

He stilled at my words. "I...we're having a baby? You are bearing me an heir? I mean I knew you were tired and your body was changing but I just assumed that you were adjusting to life down here in the Underworld. I never imagined a child!" he said in shock.

Not knowing why I blurted out, "Are you angry with me? We never talked about children..."

My words were cut short as Hades' mouth captured mine and he pulled me even closer. I wiggled in his hold so that I was straddling his lap.

"Why would I be angry at such a precious gift as a child?" I shrugged and his face showed concern. "I now have a chance to be a father. I just hope that I can be a better father than Kronos or my brothers. Never in all of my existence did I even fathom the idea of being blessed in this way. I was grateful just to have you, now I get to have you plus another. A child that I'm sure will favor both of us."

He laid me over on the couch, slinking downward, "What are you doing?" I giggled.

"I'm going to worship your body and thank it for the gift it's bearing." He trailed light kisses across my skin as he exposed it, "Just. For. Me."

Again I asked Rose and Lily, "Are you sure that my offerings will be enough to please them?"

"Yes, Mistress, you mustn't worry yourself so. It isn't good for the baby," Lily cautioned.

As we approached a voice calls for us to enter. "Allow me, my Queen." Rose walked in first, when she glanced around she waved us inside.

"Welcome, Persephone, Queen of the Underworld and goddess of Spring."

It wasn't hard to tell them apart. Clotho spun the "thread" of human fate, Lachesis dispensed it, and Atropos cut the thread, thus determining the individual's moment of death. They weaved their hands through thousands of threads.

"You knew I was coming?" I asked.

"We know everything," they said in unison. The way they mostly spoke at once was eerie in its own way.

"I have brought offerings to you all in hopes you can tell me the fate of mine and Hades' child."

Clotho searched the threads until she came across a pair of intertwined threads, one black and one white. "Sisters! Have a look at this here!"

Lachesis and Atropos hovered, studying the unique pair of threads, whispering amongst themselves.

Atropos turned about, "We accept your offering, young Queen."

"Yes," Lachesis jumped in, "You will bear Hades' twins, daughters. One of night and one of light, each taking their rightful place."

Clothos brow furrowed, "But you will have strife and trouble. You angered a god and there will be retribution unless..."

Zeus...

I paced back and forth nervously, "Unless what? How do I keep my children safe?" I pleaded. "Please, you must tell me."

"They must be hidden until they come of age, if not?" Atropos held up the scissors with their thread between the blades.

"Fine! I will hide them away. We will protect them. Thank you," I said, turning away, trying not to anger them by overstaying my welcome.

As we headed out the door, Clothos spoke up, "Young Queen, don't you want to know the rest?"

"The rest of what?" I asked.

"Of their destiny? Without their powers, they will be as weak as mortals. Make your decisions wisely with them. That's all we can say, you may be on your way now," Clothos answered as they went back to their threads, weaving and deciding fates of the humans and demigods.

Rose leaned over to Lily and whispered as we made our way down the stairs, "I heard that they have a special hidden place just for the threads of life for the original gods and goddesses."

I paused, glancing back at Rose in contempt, "Sorry, my Lady."

"Come, we have much to do to prepare for the long road ahead of us. Lily, we must summon Hecate as well," I commanded, taking off to find my mother. She and Hecate are cunning. They will help Hades and I come up with a plan.

HADES

"What do you mean she went to speak with The Fates?" I ask as Hecate finishes telling me why she visited the human realm.

"Hades, please don't make me repeat myself."

"Fine. What did they tell her?"

I watch Hecate struggle for words, "They told her that the child will be in grave danger until it comes into its powers around its tenth birthday."

My ears ring as her words sink in, and my heart shatters.

As the god of death, there is no shortage of those who dislike me, but I never imagined this kind of situation. *Who would dare hurt a child? Even if they were trying to get to me...*

"What do we do?" I questioned.

Hecate looks everywhere but my eyes as she fidgets with the hem of her shirt.

"Hecate?"

"You're not going to like it."

"As if I like any of this?"

Taking a deep fortifying breath, she takes the shattered pieces of my heart and pours salt into the wound. "Plans are in motion to hide the child in the human world until its tenth birthday."

The temperature in the room plummets, and my vision blurs. I struggle to take a single breath as everything starts spinning around me. My knees give out and I collapse in a heap on the floor.

ZEUS

My day went from bad to worse. Why is it that my wife feels the need to meddle in everyone else's business but her own? It's like she thrives on drama and gossip. To make matters worse, she always feels the need to share every detail with me. I could care less who is doing what. Unless there is a new brothel opening up in Olympus that needs business, I don't want to be bothered.

As she rambles on and on about the couples of Olympus, I roll my eyes, "You haven't mentioned

Persephone yet. Don't you have some dirt on her you'd like to share?"

Her brows furrow as she thinks about it. "Why would you say that?"

"I'm just surprised you don't have baby fever or something." I shrug.

"Why would Persephone give me baby fever?"

"Because every time another goddess gets knocked up you all but beg me for another baby." It's really quite annoying. Can't I just blow my load and be done with it? Do we really need to add more children into the mix? I don't even like the ones we already have.

Hera gasps, "Persephone is pregnant?"

"Uh, yeah. I figured everyone would know by now."

"No, no one has said a word about it and I guarantee if they knew it would have spread like wildfire." She narrows her eyes, "How is it that you came into this information?"

I shrug, "Just heard it somewhere, I guess." The truth is that I happened to be watching as she left the underworld as winter turned to spring, but I don't need to tell Hera that.

Why wouldn't my brother have told anyone yet about his wife's pregnancy? There was no doubt that Persephone had a baby bump when she left. Even I could tell that she was with child.

DEMETER

"No, absolutely not!"

"But mother, he deserves to know about them. He *is* their father!" Persephone argues.

I stand my ground. "No. You cannot tell him any details. He already knows too much. The Fates said they must be kept hidden, that includes from their father."

She rubs her large belly, as tears stream down her face, "I hate that I can't even tell him that it's twins. I feel like a horrible wife."

"I'm not trying to be callous. I know this has been hard on both of you, but it is important that we do what's best for those babies. Our lands are protected. I can add barriers and keep everyone out, but you have to continue as if nothing has changed. When you go to the underworld, you must act as though you do not have children. It will be hard, especially since you won't be able to share precious details with your husband, but we must keep them safe," I insist.

"But mother, it'll be ten years before he can see them, how can I not tell him about them?"

"Do you honestly believe it would be easier on him to know that he not only has one child he cannot see, but two? To know that you will need him even more as you try to juggle motherhood not only as a new mother but a new mother of two, living half her life separate from him. How will that help him?"

"I don't know how to do this," she sobs.

Wrapping my arms around her, I do my best to comfort her as she purges herself of her fears and misery. "It's okay. I'll be here to help you every step of the way. No matter what, we will keep these babies safe," I promise.

My poor girl has already been through so much, it pains me to see her hurting like this. It's bad enough she is cursed to spend half of the year away from the love of her life, and now she cannot even truly experience the joy of motherhood without the added worry of The Fates words.

I know that Hades would do everything in his power to protect his children, but if the wrong person were to overhear him discussing his children or see them in the underworlds during the fall and winter months, they could be in further danger. The Fates did not give specifics so it is prudent that we take every precaution afforded to us.

PERSEPHONE

Ten months went by in the blink of an eye, I couldn't quite believe how fast it all went by. I hated that because of the curse I had to spend what should have been mine and Hades' most joyous times apart from one another.

Rose and Lily were getting the dry linens ready and warming bowls of water as my mother rubbed my back singing to me. My swollen feet were dipped in the cool water of the River Styx as Thetis stood nearby to assist with the birth of our children. This was Thetis' blessing to myself and Hades. The waters of the River Styx are enchanted. It will add an extra layer of protection.

My stomach tightened and I grinded my teeth together, moaning out in pain as my mother counted the seconds out loud.

"You hear that, Thetis?" my mother smiled.

"Oh yes, the babies are on their way now," she agreed delightfully.

Then I felt it, the shift in my pelvic bone and the burning sensation that followed along with it. Vines shot out around us, creating a private grove as they twisted around one another so that no one could bear witness.

"It's time. They are coming!" I screamed out in pain.

Everyone helped me wade out into the natural spring, Lily and Rose supported my legs holding me upright as my mother wrapped her arms around my chest from behind, comforting me.

"You need to push, your Majesty. It's time," Thetis commanded.

The pain was too much to bear and I found myself weeping and crying out, "I can't. I need Hades. Hades should be here with me."

"You know he cannot be or you two would suffer something far worse than the punishment already laid out before you. Now you need to be strong for your husband and for your babies. PUSH, KORE! PUSH NOW!" mother ordered.

Grunting, I pushed with all my might, the first of my children slipping out of my womb and into Thetis' waiting hands. She came out of the water feisty and screaming at the top of her lungs as Rose took her out of the water to tend to her.

I laid back in my mother's arms relieved, I survived. "That wasn't so bad," I laughed weakly when another sharp pain hit me, causing me to double over in pain.

"Kore? What's wrong?" my mother asked worriedly, "Thetis, what's happening?'

The burning sensation returned as the words escaped me, refusing to come but Thetis was calm and collected, smiling at us. "It seems the second baby is in distress, your Majesty. We need to deliver her as soon as possible. I know you're tired, but I need you to push again."

I looked at my mother horrified. I couldn't think clearly. All I could think about was pushing, and birthing my second baby safely. The pressure was overwhelming, this child was bigger than the first one. My whole body shook, threatening to give way until the little bugger was released from my womb.

I floated on my back, allowing my mother to support my head above water. There was no sound coming from the second child, Thetis turned away from us.

"Why isn't the baby crying? Is the baby okay?" Thetis didn't answer, "Please no, no, no. Thetis!" I screamed at her.

The baby screamed out in answer as Thetis turned back towards me. "This one likes holding onto the thin line of life and death a little too much, my Queen. But she will be just fine," Thetis answered.

"She's okay? They are both okay?" I whispered in awe.

"Yes, your Majesty," Thetis confirms with a smile.

"Twins, healthy granddaughters! I am a lucky grandmother!" Demeter praised them as they helped me to wade back to shore so that I could get cleaned up and hold my babies.

With my chest bared, they were placed, one at each breast to feed. Both are as different as night and day. Happily, I announced, "Our older daughter will be called Macaria and her sister will be called Melinoe."

Chapter 4

HADES

10 Years Later...

The Underworld, the place of eternal night, was radiant in its beauty. Sure the sun held its own splendor but not like that of the night. The stars and moon shone an iridescent glow. Flowers began to take life throughout the region. From the bay of my window in the high tower, I can see the colors of their petals, as they brighten the area. A gift from Persephone, signaling her excitement that the Autumn solstice was right around the corner.

First hues of yellow, white, and pink, the Moonflowers and Evening Primroses, begin to spring up throughout the Underworld, bringing life to it and showing the souls that there was beauty to the afterlife. They gave off a glow beneath the Underworld's starry sky. A warmth spread through my cold heart, knowing my love was only a breath away.

The Queen was coming home for our half of

the year together and the Underworld was abuzz with talk of seeing their beloved Queen again. As life personified, she brought much joy to the people and souls below. My breath was taken away when a new flower started appearing down the streets and alleys until they spread around the high tower of our home.

I rushed down the stairs to meet my Queen at the entrance. While my brothers ran amuck in the realm, laying with mortal women above, my heart remained only for one. This visit was far different from any other, this would be a once in a lifetime moment and I could hardly contain my excitement; much less my nerves and anxiety. I struggled to find air when she removed her veil from her face and I rushed to embrace her in my arms.

"Hades, my love. Oh, how I have missed you!" she whispered.

"I have been counting down the days until I could hold you in my arms once more," I confessed. "What are these new creations that you have brought to the people of the Underworld this time, my love?"

"I call them Night Gladiolus. They are quite

the sight, are they not? They bloom in all colors and they smell delightful." Her smile glowed under the stars, I noticed how she held herself differently this time.

"Did you...did you bring her?" I asked quietly.

Persephone giggled at me, "My Lord, I brought them both."

"Both?" I replied confused.

She nodded signaling to her ladies, "My Lord, may I present to you, your daughters: Macaria, goddess of blessed death and Melinoe, the goddess of nightmares and madness as the Fates have foretold."

The young twins, my daughters, were brought before me and I was in awe of their beauty much less how yin and yang the two were to one another. Macaria with her long, white, straight hair and silver eyes then Melinoe stared at me with blackened eyes and long, wavy, ink-black hair.

I held out my arms to embrace them as they hesitated. Hecate stepped out from the shadows. "It's okay, girls. Your father is not to be feared and has longed for this day for over a decade."

Meekly they wrapped their arms around me,

I could feel the relief as their shoulders sunk. I looked to Persephone with a joy I could barely contain.

"A gift to mark such a joyous family union finally!" Persephone declared as she turned to the yard and knelt to the ground, placing her hands on the deadened soil.

A tree began to sprout upwards reaching as high as the tower I resided in. The bark was all different shades of the rainbow, the branches twisted and grew outwards, a work of art.

"What is it?" I asked in awe.

"I call it a Rainbow Eucalyptus tree. I came up with the idea in the Philippines and perfected it over the years. I felt like our home could use one as well," she smiled.

Macaria tugged on my shirt, "Father, why were we kept in hiding all these years?"

I bent down to meet her eye level, "Because things can be complicated in the world of gods and goddesses. Your mother and I, as well as Auntie Hecate, had to keep you safe. After your mother consulted The Fates when she was pregnant with you, their warning was clear that you were not safe. It was predicted that you would be in great danger until you came into your powers fully. Now that you have become young ladies, it should be safe for you two to come out of hiding. In fact, we are going to spend the day of solstice together in Arcadia. It's time the rest of the community knows about the princesses of the Underworld."

Persephone adds, "Girls, we talked about this. In order to keep you safe, Daddy couldn't know any more about you. There are those who would try to hurt you and we couldn't let that happen."

Hecate pushed her way between the three of us, taking my daughters into her arms. "Ugh. Enough of the serious chit-chatter, Hades! Let this Auntie *AND* Godmother see her beautiful nieces!" she scolded.

The girls giggled at her theatrics.

I turn to Persephone, while Hecate plays with the girls, "I'm afraid, I must apologize. I only have one room prepared for them." I feel so ashamed that I didn't even know I had two children. All this time, I was pining for my daughter without even realizing I had two. I feel like an awful parent.

"They sleep in the same bed still, so as long

as it is a big comfy bed, they will be happy," Persephone says reassuringly.

"The bed is as big as the one we share," I responded.

"I'm sorry about all the secrecy," she says quietly.

"We can talk about that some other time. Right now, I want to enjoy our first time together as a family."

If I'm being honest, I can't take my eyes off of my beautiful daughters. To think that we made them. It's such a profound feeling to know that the love you share with the other half of your soul could come together in such a magnificent way.

I've missed so much. I can't help but acknowledge the ache in my chest at the realization of just how much I have truly missed.

As I'm lost in thought, my lovable Cerberus comes bounding into the room. He has grown significantly over the years, from a small pup, to a full-grown beast that towers over me with his three drooling heads. I worry that his appearance could scare the girls.

I watch in fascination as the giant ball of energy I am used to, does a total personality one-eighty. He approaches calmly, lowering himself to the floor by his feet. His heads rest on the floor as his tail wags happily. It's as if he understands how important they are and he wants to show them his best side.

Before I can reassure them that he won't hurt them, the girls descend on him, petting and talking to the lovable dog. Three heads lick at each of the girls, causing them both to giggle uncontrollably. *I've never heard anything more beautiful.*

Melinoe hops on Cerberus' back. I can tell she is going to be my animal lover. She will definitely keep me on my toes. Macaria nuzzles each head in turn, showing the beast all the love in her heart.

Cerberus rises to his feet, and I hold my breath as I watch Melinoe grab onto his collars before he bounds off through the house. Melinoe's joyful cheers and giggles follow, and I do my best to remain calm.

Looking to my beloved, I check to see if she is showing any signs of concern. Until I have been able to act as a father for some time, I will need to take my queues from Persephone. If she isn't concerned that our daughter is riding a giant three-headed dog, then I will do my best to remain calm.

Macaria looks around the spacious living room. Her eyes light up when she spots the large built-in bookcases that are filled to the brim. Tilting her head, she reads the spines of several before reaching for one. It is on a shelf just out of reach so I walk over to assist.

She smiles up at me. "Could you please lift me up?"

"Absolutely, my love." My heart melts at her sweet innocence. "Do you like to read?" I ask as I set her down after she made her choice.

Nodding her head quickly, she says, "I love to read." Looking around the room she frowns. "Is there somewhere with more light that I could read this?"

"Hmm, let's see." I think about her question and realize that I need to create a room specifically for her to read in. "There is a lot of light in the office if you'd like to go in there. Tomorrow, I'll have some special lights installed for you."

"Thank you, I think I'll stay here for now if that's okay," she says quietly.

"Of course. Wherever you are most

comfortable."

I want to tell her I love her and that I will do anything to make her happy, even if it means bringing a million watts of light into a room for her, but I know that it is too soon for her. She just met me and although I can feel my bond with her and her sister already, I know it doesn't always work that quickly for children. They've been sheltered their entire life. Taught not to trust strangers, and that is exactly what I am to them right now. One day I will be a father to them, not just biologically but emotionally as well. I just have to be patient.

One conversation, one shared interest, one day at a time.

PERSEPHONE

Nothing compares to the love I witnessed in Hades' eyes when he finally got to meet his daughters. I'm sure later on he will have questions about why I didn't tell him they were twins. He knew about my visit to see The Fates, but I had left out the fact that there were two. I'll explain eventually why my mother and I felt it was so imperative to keep it all hush hush, even if that meant not telling him of our other daughter.

With Hades distracted, I wandered over to Hecate who was observing Hades trying to build a relationship with our daughters. With Melinoe, it was easy because they were two peas in a pod but with Macaria? It was a bit harder considering she was more like me than him.

Melinoe was all about the grim melancholy things of life. She preferred stormy days over ones filled with sunshine. If you want to see her smile? Watch how she reacts to a tornado making its way across a field at full force.

Macaria on the other hand loved to bask in the sunlight, pick flowers, and play music. She's never mean and all who come into contact with her love her. Melinoe is introverted and loves her books full of fantasy stories that she can use to escape away from the realities of this world.

"My Queen, you seem troubled on such a joyous occasion?" Hecate said concerned.

"Just worried is all, I'm always worried. Always questioning myself or watching over my shoulder. Cautiously second-guessing anyone I come into contact with and even those I know," I mumble on without thinking.

Hecate gave me a look of suspicion, "Is someone bothering you in the mortal realm, your Highness?"

I stilled, knowing I had given myself away. I had finally let my paranoia get the best of me but I had to keep my mouth shut. What would Hades do if he found out? Would he still want me? Our girls? Would he question the legitimacy of our children? Questions, doubts, and fear started to overrun my mind all at once. I felt dizzy from the sudden onslaught of panic and anxiety as my vision started to blur and even darken around the edges.

Hecate caught me as I stumbled a bit, "I'm sorry. I think I am just overcome with all of the excitement of the day of reuniting with Hades and introducing him to the girls," I lied.

"Kore? Are you okay, my love?" Hades asked, his face full of concern.

I waved him off, "Yes, love. The journey has just taken a bit out of me. Hecate was just helping me to go lie down for a while. Please, you all continue having fun. I'll catch up with you all in a few hours after I've rested."

Letting Hecate lead the way, I'm guided to the sitting room that is connected to the bedroom I share with Hades.

"Now that we're alone, I think it's time you tell me about what has you all worked up. There should be no fear or paranoia since the time that The Fates have predicted has passed."

"But has it? Has it really passed? Are they truly safe now?" I questioned, leaning back onto the couch. I worry every day that I misinterpreted their warning. *Should I have kept them hidden longer?*

Plopping down across from me, Hecate gave me a no-nonsense look. "Persephone, everyone is on high alert now that the princesses are home. Orders have been issued and they have personal bodyguards, including their ladies that follow them around like flies to a corpse. No one is going to even breathe in their direction without any of us knowing."

"I know, I know. I'm just worried is all. I can't help it," I whispered.

"Why don't you tell me about who has been stalking you?" she asked. I opened my mouth to protest and lie but she held up her hand refusing to argue. "Your Highness, I have been around for many centuries. In my long-lived life, I know that there is no way that there has not been a single god, demi-god, or mortal man that would not try to sway your eyes away from Hades. Whether for your looks, to ruin you, or to try and use you for your position for their gain. I know it had to have happened at least once because we are women and that's how our fortune goes. But what I can offer you is comfort and support, maybe even a little revenge. If you tell me, whoever it is will never bother you again. This is part of my job in the underworld as Hades' right hand. Let me do the same for you, my Lady."

Tears welled up in my eyes, I've been holding it in all these years but I couldn't ignore the pull that was telling me to keep my mouth shut. So I went with a half-truth instead, "It was just some man-child asshole that came to the Temple and roused my anger because he praised Zeus after saying I was unworthy. He said we failed him and the villagers when we didn't. I punished him...and the other villagers. I let my anger get the best of me, but Demeter helped me set things in order. She walked with me through the village as we blessed the fields individually. Those who chose to mock us were bypassed as their families watched on in fear."

I watched as Hecate visibly relaxed at my confession, "Well it sounds like that pompous ass got what he deserved to me. I'm glad your mother helped you handle it but I must say I am surprised by your chaotic side of your goddessship."

"Yeah, everything was amplified, including my temper, it seems. I blame it on hormones," I winked, joking.

"Well get some rest, your Highness. There is much to do in your time at home," Hecate smiled while turning to walk out.

Once the door closed and her footsteps faded down the hallway, my chest sank and the weight of my tears came crashing down around me. I cannot afford to allow myself this moment of weakness, not if I intend for my secret to remain just that, a secret. Coming to my feet, I decided to draw myself a hot bath. The heat and humidity will hide my tears and give me time to pull myself together before my husband finds me.

Chapter 5
HADES

For years, my family has been living this odd rhythm of six months together and six apart. We came up with a new plan once I was finally able to see my girls. I couldn't be the kind of father I wanted to be while spending so much time away from my girls. I missed ten years of their lives due to the cautionary words of The Fates, and I refused to lose even more time. Hecate and Demeter agreed to coordinate transportation between worlds. My wife and I may not be able to see one another during the spring and summer months but there was no restriction in place for our children.

I worried that our arrangements would be detrimental for our girls, spending one week with their mother then the next with me and so on, but they seemed to thrive. Maybe it's wishful thinking or the delusions of a father, but our children are happy. Now they are entering adulthood, and I couldn't be prouder of the young women they have become.

As Persephone walks out of our master bathroom, fresh from her shower, I can't help but picture what lies beneath that towel. Even after all this time, I feel as if it's our first night together. Her mere presence ignites a thirst inside of me, one that can only be quenched by her touch.

Today had been a long day of preparations for the girls' debutante party, so I wasn't able to spend as much time with my wife as I would have liked.

"I missed you today, my love," I say as I walk over to her.

She smiles, blushing slightly, "I missed you today too. I didn't realize how much work this party was going to be."

"It is, but you've handled it spectacularly."

"I had a lot of help."

"That may be so, but I still think you deserve a reward for all your effort," I say as I lean in to kiss her neck.

"A reward, huh? And what kind of reward did you have in mind?" she asks breathlessly.

"Oh, I think you know, but how about I show you?" In one swift motion, her towel falls to the floor.

Sinking to my knees in front of her, I rub my hands across her sensitive skin until I'm holding the soft flesh of her behind. Without hesitation, I lean in to kiss her along her pubic bone, making my way closer and closer to her core. I suck and nibble until Persephone is pulling on my hair, begging me for more.

"You want more, my love?" I ask against her skin.

"I need you," she pants.

"Well, why didn't you say that in the first place?" I tease.

"Hades," she whines.

In one fluid motion, I rise from the floor and lift her into my arms. Walking over to the bed, with Persephone in my arms, she manages to pull my shirt over my head, tossing it who knows where. I set her on the edge of the bed and remove my pants and boxer briefs. She tries to scoot further up the bed, but I grasp her ankles and pull her back to the edge.

She gasps, but doesn't protest.

Bending over, I lavish first one nipple, then the other. Once I have her moaning my name again, I position myself between her legs and enter her in one swift motion. With her legs wrapped around me, and my feet placed solidly on the floor, I have added leverage and I'm able to pound into her harder than in missionary. I also get a glorious view of her breasts as they bounce with each thrust. My grip on her hips will definitely leave marks, but she doesn't protest.

Using her body language and moans as a guide, I increase my speed and the force behind each and every time I enter her. My sweet little goddess of spring and life likes it rough, and I am more than willing to oblige.

Our bodies glisten with the evidence of our excursion. The beads of sweat roll down my chest and onto her. There is no doubt, we will both need to shower after the night is over. Then again, we'll probably need a shower *after* the shower as well.

I feel her core tightening around my hard length and I know she is close. Releasing one hip, I reach forward to pinch her nipple. The added sensation sends her over the edge. As she screams my name, I have to return my grip on her hip as my own release barrels through me.

Bracing myself, I try to catch my breath before I can pull out.

"You keep making love to me like that and we'll have another baby on the way in no time," she says between breaths.

I know she meant it as a joke, but at the mere mention of knocking her up again, I'm ready for another round. I'd love to have more children with her, even if our circumstances are less than desirable.

DEMETER

How is it that my granddaughters are already of age? It feels like just yesterday that their mother was reborn and now here we are, planning their coming of age party. They will officially be presented in front of all the other gods and goddesses of Olympus and the Underworld. It's terrifying to know that they will no longer be kept sheltered from the rest of the worlds.

Despite the fact that The Fates' warning has long passed, I still worry for their safety. Many gods and goddesses could see them as a way of getting to either of their parents.

"Do you think we are doing the right thing?" my daughter asks, nervously.

Tilting my head, I ask, "By having their party here in South Carolina?"

"By having a party at all." She paces back and forth in the small dining room where we have been going over the final details for the event.

"It is tradition, my dear, plus the girls are so excited. Well, one of them is."

Persephone laughs at the reference to how different her girls are, like night and day in every sense of the word. One shy and quiet, the other vocal and outgoing. One prefers the night, while the other embraces the sunshine and all it has to offer. They may be twins by birth and a shared womb, but their similarities stop there.

"I just wish I could keep them hidden and protected forever," Persephone admits.

"I know you do, my dear Daughter, but that is no way to live life. They need to be able to make their own decisions and find their own paths in life. It won't happen overnight, but their strength will grow with each passing day and you will be able to rest assured that they will be able to take care of themselves."

"I worry about them."

"And that will never change, not ever. You are their mother. You will always worry over your babies, but you can't let that stop you from living your own life while they live theirs. They know that you are here if they need you," I reassure her.

"What if something happens and I'm not there to help them?"

"Then your husband will, or their godmother or their grandmother. They are not alone in this life."

Persephone nods, but still looks worried.

"It's just a party. It's not like they are moving out or leaving. Take a deep breath, my dear."

She sighs, "You're right. Thank you, Mother."

PERSEPHONE

All of the gods of Olympia were in attendance for our girls coming-of-age party. I had barely allowed the girls out of my sight, even with them coming of age and entering adulthood tonight; that only made the worry that much worse for me as a mother. Now that they were adults, they were at risk of any and every bad thing happening to them.

"Dance with me, my love," Hades whispered in my ear.

I glanced away at the girls, "Maybe later after the girls have gone to bed?"

Hades chuckled, "My love, those young ladies are having the time of their lives," he paused slightly then we both broke out in laughter. "Yeah, they're not going anywhere until I force them to slumber."

I exhaled a deep breath and groaned, "You're probably right."

Taking his hands, the floor cleared as we made our way to the center. Music played a familiar tune as Hades guided me across the floor in old steps we have taken many a night alone in our bedroom.

Hades gazed upon me with a new twinkle in his eyes, "The Underworld and I have missed you, my Queen."

I smiled, "As I have missed them. Did you like the new additions I've created for the Underworld?"

"Ah yes. I think the souls and subjects will have much joy." His breathing became unsteady as he leaned down, "Dare I say that I am ready to have you in my bed. We could just...disappear. No one would notice our absence." He shrugged, waggling his eyebrows at me.

"Hades!" I gasped slapping his chest playfully which only caused him to squeeze me tighter to his chest. "You are quite the scoundrel every time I come home."

He leaned his lips down to mine, "For you? I would do anything, be anything, just to spend another moment in your arms."

I couldn't help but notice, out of peripheral, that Hera and Zeus were eyeballing us. An uneasy feeling washed over my entire being, I felt physically ill at the moment. Something wasn't right. Or maybe just off? I couldn't quite place it.

Leaning into Hades' ears, "What's with Zeus and Hera? Why are they staring at us like that?"

Hades turned his head towards them and stiffened, "I don't know. Maybe they are fighting again?"

I giggled, "Oh? Did the King of Olympia take on a new mistress again?"

He rolled his eyes and shrugged in disgust, "When does he *not* have a new mistress?"

Taking Hades hand in mine, I pulled him from the dance floor and headed over for refreshments. Hecate was barking orders at some nymphs but straightened up when we came over.

Handing us a couple of glasses of mead, she smiled and glanced back at the nymphs working diligently.

"Hecate...you really outdid yourself for the girls' party. This is extravagant to say the least," I praise.

Hecate blushed, "Anything for my goddaughters. Well, I can't take *all* the credit. Your mother helped me out quite a bit with the details to help feature the world above as much as much as the world below."

"Speaking of which, where did the girls get off to?" I questioned looking around.

The hairs on the back of my neck stood up when I noticed that Zeus and Hera were no longer present and my heart sank, skipping a few beats as I snatched onto Hades' arm.

"Something's wrong. We need to find the girls, now!" I cried.

"My love, calm down. I'm sure they're around here somewhere." Hades tried to reassure me, but the look in his eyes told me he was just as concerned.

Turning about and looking him in the eyes, there was a small gasp from both Hades and Hecate, "My queen...your eyes."

I looked down at my reflection in the tray, red eyes stared back at me. "Find. My. Daughters. Now!" I commanded.

Hecate nodded as we all separated looking around the banquet hall for them. It was hard to remember that we were in the human world right now so as gods, goddesses and other worldlies we were to remain invisible in the sense that no humans could see our true forms.

Frantically, Hades and Hecate asked the staff and pleaded with them to help me find my daughters. My legs felt like jelly refusing to move. Closing my eyes, I focused all of my energy on them. It was a last-ditch effort to feel something of our remaining bond that we had left. As their mother, I have a special bond with them that allows me to find their location, but the bond dissipates as children come into their own powers. My efforts felt like they were in vain, my mind became muddled as if trying to wade through muddy water. I could feel their life force but that was it, like they were just out of reach.

"ARGHHH!" I screamed out as black smoke escaped from my fingertips in search of what I had lost.

In an instant, Hades was by my side, "Kore, you have to stop or you will destroy this world," he warned.

Clenching my fist, I banged them against my knees, unable to contain the rage that was quickly becoming out of control. My girls were gone, someone must have taken them. That much was clear.

"I should have never allowed them out of hiding, they barely know their powers and what they're capable of," I sobbed.

Hades hugged me close to his chest, "What makes you so sure that someone has taken them?"

Guilt gripped at my heartstrings, plucking them one by one but still I lied, "We live in a world of gods and goddesses who do terrible things if someone just looks at them wrong. The Fates felt the need to warn us. Need I say more?"

Hades' brow furrowed, "Good point."

Hecate and Poseidon rushed to our side, Hermes following closely behind, his face looked full of guilt as if he murdered my dog.

Trembling, he held out a note to me and Hades, "This was left on the emergency exit with these as well."

With his other hand, Hermes handed me the girls' Forget-Me-Not hair clips, one that was white while the other was black.

With hands that shook, I studied the penmanship on the paper. *Did I know it?* Or was my mind playing deceitful tricks on me. Unable to open the folded paper, a simple task at most, Hades gently pried the thin slip from my hands. Taking a deep breath he did what I could not and opened the note.

Out loud her read:

You won't find them so don't even bother trying. I've taken them somewhere that no one can find them. Once their powers have been drained, I will provide further instruction on their return. If I receive word that you left your positions to search for them then I will kill them. Be grateful that I am only taking their powers.

"There's no indication of who took them in this note, only that they plan to drain their powers," Hades complained frustrated.

"Hades, that would make them...human," I gasped in horror at the realization of what would happen to them if we didn't find them in time. My sanity was hanging on by a thread at this point. With no idea of what else to do, I started pacing, "I will *not* stand idly by while some psycho drains our daughters of their powers for whatever reason. Plus there is no promise that no other harm will come to them!" I shuddered at the thought of my daughters being taken advantage of by some god.

I had no proof but the only one with any issues with me was Zeus, apparently the king could hold a grudge longer than I imagined. *This is all my fault*, if I had just given into his advances he would never have bothered my family. Bad things always happen to women who refuse him, human and goddess alike.

"Whoever this is must have eyes everywhere," Poseidon mumbled.

"Like Zeus?" Hecate connected the dots thankfully.

Hades swiped his hand to the side, "My brother wouldn't dare challenge me, let alone threaten my children."

"Your brother is jealous of everything he can't have, mostly his fault as a womanizer but that's beside the point. He's a narcissist at its finest." Hecate looked over at Poseidon before cutting her eyes at him, "I dare you to tell him what I said."

Poseidon visibly gulped before leaving the room. I loved that some goddesses were to be feared in some way.

"It's possible but in all actuality, we have no clue as to where to start looking or who to investigate. Hades, where do we start?"

"The place where all humans and gods go to seek out help. *The Fates.*"

"But how? The note says we can't leave," I ask, terrified for my daughters.

"I think Hecate and I can handle that part," Proteus chimes in.

Within an hour, a plan was devised. Hecate and Proteus would alter their appearance in order to look like us, allowing Hades and I to seek guidance from The Fates.

Chapter 6
HADES

How could this happen? How could someone just take the girls without one of us realizing? As much as I hate to entertain the thought, it had to be someone we know, someone we trusted. Our girls wouldn't wander far, and they definitely wouldn't go willingly with anyone they didn't know. They know the dangers.

Seeing Persephone on the verge of losing control like that is something I'll never forget. We've talked about her fear of losing control in the past, but I had never seen the change in her first hand before. I'm sure there is more to it than simply a change of eye color, but the fact that she was that shaken means we have to hurry. She is a mother through and through, any intuition she has is not to be ignored.

When she first mentioned not seeing the girls, I hadn't been too concerned because they could have easily been in the restroom or chatting with a relative. But when I saw Persephone stiffen, I knew her intuition had triggered an instinctive response. We need to find our girls and fast. I can't bear the thought of them in danger.

One thing is for certain, those responsible will pay! My own anger is a force to be reckoned with. No one touches what is mine and gets away with it.

Taking a deep, calming breath, I do my best to maintain control over my rage. After we find our girls there will be plenty of time for me to exact my revenge.

Wearing our hooded capes, Persephone and I make the climb up the rocky mountainside to the Cave of Fates. The path is harsh and long, intended to minimize the number of visitors inquiring about trivial things. Only those who are willing to make the journey will be given consideration.

The Fates

"You were granted a warning, one which you did not heed. Now the knowledge you seek requires a steep price. We will not simply tell you, for the treasures you seek are far more valuable than you could imagine."

Hades' eyes flash with anger, "We did heed your warning! We kept them hidden until they came into their powers, how were we to know-"

"SILENCE!" We cut him off before he can anger us, forcing us to change our minds.

We watch as Persephone places a comforting hand on her husband's arm. The worry and fear is written all over her expression. Good. A concerned mother will do anything in her power to save her children.

"For the information you seek, tasks you must complete. Favor is not granted at the will of a god or goddess. Blessings must be earned, even blessings in the form of aid."

"Anything. We will do anything to get our girls back," Persephone pleads.

Hades wisely remains silent next to her, but his eyes mirror her candor.

Nodding, we gather the supplies we will need to bind our agreement. First, a candle lit with the flame from the furthest depths of the underworld. Second, a handful of dust collected from the darkest regions of space where creation began. The third and final element being a pair of differing hairs, one the mother of land and life, the other the father of death and the underworld.

With swift plucks, the hairs are twisted together. "Hold hands," we instruct.

As they do as they are told, we bind their wrists with the hairs. Carefully the dust is placed on their clasped hands. We use the candle to ignite the hairs. As the flame burns bright, it works its way around their wrists. Remarkably, neither flinch at the heat. Once the flame has incinerated the hairs, the dust catches fire, glowing with a brilliant blue flame. The flame flares several inches above their joined hands before extinguishing, sealing our covenant.

"And so it shall be, by the power of three, past, present, and future, we bind thee to We."

"What do we need to do?" Hades asks through clenched teeth.

It takes great courage to face The Fates and speak to us in such a manner. It takes even greater courage to bind oneself to our tasks without prior knowledge of what they may be. We respect their pure and unconditional love for their children.

"Balance must be maintained in all things. For three lives, three tasks must be completed. Three wrongs must be made right. Over the eons of existence, gods and goddesses have caused quite a great deal of chaos."

"That's an understatement," Persephone scoffs sarcastically before she can stop herself.

We can't help but smile at the young goddess, she has such purity within her, despite the violence and rage dancing alongside that innocence.

"Your first task is to rescue Medusa."

"But she-" Hades starts to say, but we stop him.

"Yes, we know, but you will find a way. Second, you will free the Minotaur from Midas' maze. Once you have successfully completed the first two tasks, you will then retrieve Amalthea's horn. Your tasks must be completed in order and swiftly. Time is not on your side."

"I mean no offense, but how will we know where to find our girls? I worry that time is not on their side either," Persephone asks.

"Each task will lead you to the next. Upon completion, all will be made clear."

"Wait, you said three lives, but we only have two daughters?" Hades says, confused.

"All will be made clear...in due time. Now leave us. Time is not on your side."

Demeter

This whole situation is just awful! We spent so many years working hard to keep those girls safe and in one night all of it is lost. *How could this happen? How could someone have taken my granddaughters right out from under our noses?* I can think of several gods and goddesses who would benefit from such an atrocious deed but none that would have the gall to do so. It takes a lot of confidence to cross the god of death.

"I can't keep doing nothing! We need to do *something*." I complain as Hades and Persephone sit calmly at the table in the conference room. "What's the plan? You have to have a plan."

"You read the note. We cannot leave," Persephone says in an odd tone of voice.

I look at her as if she's grown two heads. "We can't do nothing!"

"We're not doing nothing," Hades says, but doesn't elaborate.

Something isn't right here. "What do you know?" I ask.

"Us? Nothing." They exchange glances before going back to playing statues.

Before I can knock some sense into them, the door opens behind me and two hooded figures enter. They quickly draw the shades so that no one can see into the conference room. As they remove their hoods, I can't believe what I'm seeing.

Standing before me is Persephone and Hades...but...but...I look between the pair sitting at the table and the pair that just entered. When I look toward the pair sitting at the table again, they've transformed into Hecate and Proteus.

Putting my fists on my hips, I let my head fall back as I take several calming breaths.

"You couldn't have filled me in on your plan? Here I am freaking out thinking you two have lost your ever-loving minds by just sitting here and not coming up with a plan and you've already got a plan in motion."

"Not exactly...I mean sort of," Persephone says.

"We went to speak with The Fates," Hades explains. "But the tasks they gave us seem...well, impossible, so we are going to need to come up with a few miracles if we are going to pull it all off in time."

"How can we help?" Hecate asks.

"We are going to need the two of you to continue to act in our stead. Whoever took them will still be watching. Beyond that, well let's sit down and talk about what we were told." He pulls a chair out for Persephone before taking the one next to her.

If there is any chance that we can find the girls before their powers are drained, we have to try. No matter how hard or impossible it may seem, we have to try.

ZEUS

"Where are we going?" Hera complained.

"Home. We have to get out of the area now," I insist.

"But I want to stay and see what happens," she whines.

"No, Hera." I grab her hand and start walking. "Nothing good can come of staying here. My brother's fury will be unmatched."

Rolling her eyes, she says, "But I heard the note said the girls wouldn't be killed."

"Their powers will be gone which makes them mortal...as mortal as Hercules. You remember how that ended."

Hera sighs heavily, "Fine, but you are going to take me to a nice restaurant. I spent a great deal of money on this dress and these shoes, the least you can do is show me off in it."

"Whatever, just get in the car."

She smiles as if she just won the grand prize and slides into the passenger side of the waiting car. When in the human world, we travel as the humans do.

Shooting through traffic, I put as much distance as I can between myself and the chaos of the kidnapping. A smile forms on my face as I think of how distraught Persephone must be. *Serves her right.* After all these years of denying me, she's finally getting what she deserves.

Chapter 7

PERSEPHONE

"Excuse me, your Majesty, but how the hell are we supposed to break Medusa's curse? Number one, she's dead and number two, Perseus beheaded her. Oh, and number three, he tossed her head into the sea after turning the Kraken to freakin stone!" Hecate pointed out while pacing back and forth while the rest of us sat around the table in the conference room.

'That's not exactly...true," Demeter mumbled.

All eyes fell on my mother who looked away nervously fidgeting in her chair. "Well you see..." she started but paused.

"Mother? Please if you know anything, you must tell us so we can find the girls faster," I pleaded.

Rubbing the back of her neck, she took a deep breath before sighing, "So the legends are true but after what Perseus had done, he was overcome with guilt. So he came to me for help, I was unsure of what I could do but he wanted her to be reborn. I informed him that I could not because I was sure Zeus or Athena would hear. You know Hera has eyes and ears everywhere in the mortal realm, so I tasked Perseus with bringing me her body and head. The least I could do was hide away her dormant corpse for protection. In order for Perseus to retrieve her head, a deal was struck with Poseidon. That's how Arion ended up coming about but that's a story for another time, I suppose."

"So where did you hide her?" Hades asked.

"In the now dormant volcano of Pompei. After it erupted and everyone died there, it was the perfect place to hide her from any god searching for her."

"A freaking volcano, Demeter?!" Hecate cried in disbelief.

"Well it seemed like a good idea at the time, Hecate!" Demeter spat. "Plus those were the days before the earth became advanced for their civilization and I didn't have many options."

"I'm going to need directions, Demeter, to the entrance where you hid her within that volcano," Hades said.

"Once you find her, she's technically dead so how do you two plan on bringing her back?" Demeter asked.

I waved her off, "The Fates said that it will all become apparent in the moment. So I'm not going to worry about it until we are face to face with the situation at hand. Once Medusa is uncursed, I'm hoping we will know what to do next." I looked towards Hades. "Let's go. Time's not on our side."

Hades and I changed our clothes and were gathering our things to head out when Lily and Rose came to us.

Raising an eyebrow, I asked, "What do you two think you're doing?"

"You didn't think you were going alone now, did you?" Lily answered.

I shook my head, "No, nope. Absolutely not, I forbid it!"

But the two of them just stood there with their arms crossed, "We're going, with or without your permission, your Highness," Rose argued.

Flustered, I exhaled, "You could die. Both of you could die, you know. This is dangerous."

"And that's why we're going with you. It's dangerous, you can use all the help you can get, now giddy up and let's get on with this shitshow while we still can. You said it yourself. Time's not on our side, your Majesty," Lily said while Rose nodded.

Without another word, Hades led us to the portal that would lead us to Medusa's resting place.

Thankfully for us as gods, it was easy to create a portal to use to get wherever we wanted in the human realm. Hades landed us right at the entrance hidden away on the upper side of the volcano.

Hades removed the drape of ivy, revealing the entrance. "We have no idea what we will be walking into. Remember that even though she's dormant, as your mother claims, we really don't know what we are walking into here."

"Right. Don't look directly at her. I think we'll be okay though. After all, my mother was able to handle her...pieces," I mused.

"It's because your mother is a woman," Rose chimes in. "The curse affects men."

We all look toward her in shock.

"What? You don't remember the story?" When no one says anything, she explains, "Athena was mad at Medusa for breaking her vow of celibacy. She had an affair with Poseidon and Athena felt she needed to be punished. Aphrodite was mad because Poseidon thought Medusa was prettier than her so they teamed up, but it was Athena who did the cursing. They decided together that no man should ever look upon Medusa again, so they turned her into the half serpent creature with snakes for hair and for added measure any man that looked upon her would turn to stone. The worst part is Athena has convinced herself that she *blessed* Medusa by giving her the ability to live her life without the dealings of men."

"Okay then. That means, Hades, you will need to stay here where you will be safe."

Hades paused from pacing back and forth and gave me a look, "I don't like this plan. Who is going to protect you?"

"We will protect her with our lives if necessary, my Lord. We swear to you, no harm will come to her," Lily vowed while Rose nodded in agreement.

Exhaling, Hades unwillingly gave in, "Fine. But if I feel like you all are taking too long then I will come in, consequences be damned."

I leaned up on tiptoes, "I would expect nothing less, my love."

Hades held my chin between his fingers, "I love you."

"I love you too," I whispered before Rose led the way into the cavern and I followed with Lily sandwiching me between them.

"I can't see a bloody thing in here. Mistress, can you help us?" Rose asked quietly.

Rubbing my hands together, I focused on the heat I felt burning between my palms as I pulled them apart from one another. A large orb of light took form before splitting into several smaller ones. Once released, they float up above our heads and take off down the corridors, illuminating our pathway.

We didn't have to walk long until we found ourselves before two separate pathways.

"Which way do we go, your Majesty?" Lily asked.

Walking around, I searched the walls and floors for any markings, "My mother is quite a cunning woman who is always underestimated by others." Moss had grown on the floor in sporadic patches. Kneeling down, I noticed small little bugs crawling towards one particular patch against the left wall.

"What is it, my Lady? Rose asked cautiously.

"I think the two pathways are a distraction or detour, see how these ants are crawling between this one particular stone?" They both nodded in acknowledgement. "Everyone get down on the ground just in case I'm wrong and this is actually a boobytrap instead.

Both of them got down on their stomachs mimicking my actions. I pushed down on the mossy stone the ants were disappearing into and the wall popped back inwards and moved to the side revealing a staircase downwards.

"Well...that was anticlimactic," Lily muttered as there was an audible clicking noise before metal arrows launched across the corridor and stuck in the wall behind us.

Rose broke out in muffled laughter, "You just had to jinx us, didn't you, Lily?"

I rolled over onto my back in an uncontrollable fit of giggles, "That was exhilarating!" The two nymphs stood up, rolling their eyes at me as they helped me to my feet.

"What? Don't judge me! I've been sheltered my whole life."

The orbs followed, lighting our path as we headed down the staircase. As the orbs continued deeper into the chamber, the clearer our path became. In the middle of the chamber laying on a stone altar, Medusa's body lay motionless. She hadn't deteriorated a bit over the centuries and still held a certain beauty about her even though her lower half is in the form of a large serpent. Her severed head was placed with care above her detached body.

"How do you plan to wake her, my Queen?" Rose asked.

"Medusa is part serpent and I am Life personified. I can give life back to her and once I do then she should return back to normal. At least, I hope for that last part."

Placing my hands on top of the stone altar, grass spread across it softening the bedding she laid on. The blades of grass worked to knit her flesh back together at the place where her head was separated from her body, making her body whole once more. I placed my hands on her shoulder, allowing life to flow from within me, to inside of her.

Her chest rose as she gasped, taking a deep breath for the first time in centuries. Her eyes slowly opened, coming alive. What I saw in their depths was not a look of relief, but rather one of defense.

Before I could react, Lily shoved me out of the way as Medusa grabbed the closest thing to her, which happened to be Lily's shoulders. Medusa's fangs latched into the soft flesh of Lily's collarbone area. She stumbled backwards before falling onto her knees, her veins blackening, the color spreading up the column of her neck and down to her chest.

"Lily, no!" I screamed as Medusa hissed from the altar, crouching in defense.

Medusa gave us a strange look before it turned to a look of horror, "I feel strange," she hissed before her body started contorting on top of the altar. Falling over the opposite side from us, we couldn't see her but could hear her agony.

"What's happening to her?" Rose asked, through her own tears.

"She's transforming back to her original self." Crawling over to Lily, Medusa was the last thing I cared about at the moment.

Cradling Lily in my lap, tears fell down my cheeks as I sobbed. "It's going to be okay, Lily. I'm going to take the poison away from you. You're going to be okay."

My hands cupped the puncture wounds trying to draw out the poison but instead it cemented refusing to leave her veins.

"Your Majesty, it's not working," Rose cried.

"No, no, no, no no!"

"Mistress. Stop," Lily whispered weakly.

"Why...why is it not working?" I shouted confused.

Lily put her hands on top of mine. "Kore. Stop. Please."

"I can't lose you! We can't lose you!" I sobbed, resting my forehead against hers. "This is all my fault. Why? Why would you sacrifice yourself? I would have been fine. Don't you know your life is worth more than mine?!"

Lily smiled weakly at me, "That is exactly why. You are worthy to die for, because I know you would have died in order for me to live." She looked over at Rose, letting one hand fall on her lap, "Take care of our queen, will you?"

She nodded, unable to speak. Lily's eyes fluttered heavily as she struggled to keep them open now. The poison was almost to her heart, it wouldn't be long now.

"Would you hum that song for me? The one that you hum when you are creating beautiful things for your creations?" she mumbled.

"Of course, Lily. Anything for you." Sniffling, I wiped my nose ungracefully on my sleeve and cleared my throat.

Holding Lily's head to my chest so she could focus on my heartbeat, the whimsical tune fell from my lips as Lily's life force started to slip away from her body. A final breath left her body as it relaxed in my arms and I knew she was gone.

"Oh my gods. I killed her," Medusa whispered in horror as she came around the altar towards us.

Rose and I glanced up from Lily's still form, staring at Medusa. I should be angry but all I felt was pity for her. She's no longer a monster, her hair that used to be snakes was now long black curls dangling around her. No more green scale-covered flesh but mocha cream skin that looked soft as a baby's bottom. Big wide green eyes stared at us, still hypnotizing to gaze upon.

Rose shot up in rage, "You dare to stand before the goddess of spring and life? Bow, you fool, and beg for forgiveness for murdering my sister!"

Medusa fell to her knees, posturing herself before me. "Your Highness, you must believe me, I had no control over my body before you transformed me. Please, don't curse me again."

Gently, I laid Lily's head down on the stone floor before standing up, "Rose, stand down. I am not harsh nor am I a cruel being."

"Sorry, Mistress," she wept, kneeling back down by Lily's body.

"Medusa. I do not blame you for what happened. We knew the risks coming here." Trying my best to place a facade across my face, I commanded, "Help me to put her on the altar."

Rose and Medusa immediately gathered Lily's body while I prepped the stone table for her. I did my best to make the moss thicker so that her back would not suffer from the stone.

Quietly, they placed her body on top, "Stand back," I commanded.

I reached for the ground, summoning the roots of a weeping willow tree. The branches came up through the floor twisting around the altar and enclosing Lily inside. Blooms and thin branches grew and drooped downward like a giant umbrella around us.

"She will never dwell in darkness, she will have sun and gaze upon the stars every night," I vowed as the volcanic walls cracked upwards until an opening appeared in the ceiling.

Rose and Medusa stepped back as I turned towards them. "Mistress, your eyes."

Refusing to say anything else, I turned away from them and headed towards the staircase. I thought I knew pain but when Lily died, it felt as though a part of me died with her.

HECATE

Gods, goddesses, and several beings from both Olympus and the Underworld pass the conference room, occasionally stopping to check on us. Proteus and I maintained our disguise as we impersonated Hades and Persephone. At this rate, we will have less eliminated as innocent then we will have actual suspects.

Demeter fields most of their inquiries, assuring them that everything that can be done, is being done in order to find the girls. She is smart to stop them at the door, making sure that we do not have to talk to anyone. A simple misstep in a conversation could easily break our cover.

I hate just sitting here doing nothing. I know it's important to have someone here so that it appears as though neither Hades or Persephone have left, but I feel helpless. These are my god-daughters we are talking about. They mean everything to me, and I can't even be out there looking for them.

When I find out who is responsible, they will beg for mercy...if their father doesn't destroy them first.

Maybe when this is all over, I'll pay a special visit to those hags that call themselves The Fates. How could they issue such riddles and impossible tasks when the girls' lives are on the line? It's not right. The Fates see all; past, present, and future. They don't deserve to hold such powerful information if they are not going to use it for good.

My frustration boils, and I have to force myself to calm down or risk my disguise slipping. Now I know what a caged animal feels like.

"Take a deep breath," Proteus urges from his seat next to me.

It's odd to see Hades' form, but know that it is someone else.

"We have to have faith that they will complete their tasks in time," he says calmly.

Demeter's knees buckle and she falls to the floor next to the closed door of the conference room. We rush to her side, but see no visible injuries.

"What's wrong?" I ask urgently.

Clutching her chest, she gasps, "Lily...Lily is gone...Lily is dead." Her eyes glisten with tears as she meets my gaze.

"How do you know?" Proteus asks.

"I created her," she responds simply.

HADES

As I pace the entrance of the cavern, I can barely contain myself as I hear the echoes of a scream from deep within. The sounds were angry at first, but quickly turned to a sorrowful sound. For a split second, I thought the worst but then I realized that if my wife were lost to this world, I'd be the first to know. As time passed, I feared I'd lose my sanity, but then I heard the softest of tunes carried upon the air flowing through the tunnels.

I knew something bad must have happened, but I didn't realize how bad until Lily's soul appeared coming from within the cavern entrance.

As Lily approached, she knelt before me, "I did all that I could, your Majesty. Persephone is no longer in danger. Please have mercy..."

"Lily, rise. You need not kneel before me. You have been not only a loyal maiden to my wife, but you have been one of her dearest friends." I look behind her, in the direction she came and I can't help but worry about the pain my dearest Persephone must be feeling right now. "I'm so sorry, Lily, but I must escort you to the other side now. Your soul cannot survive in this world. It will wither away if we delay."

She looks up at me with fear in her eyes, "I'm scared, your Majesty." Her voice comes out in barely a whisper.

"You have nothing to fear. The place you are going is one of peace and love. I think you'll find it...well, that will be for you to decide, just know that you are blessed," I say before forming a portal to ferry her soul.

In the blink of an eye, Lily's soul crosses into the afterlife, and I'm able to return to the cavern entrance. As much as I want to go to Persephone, I know that I have to let her do this on her own.

It isn't long before I see three figures walking toward me. My heart races. If Persephone is hurt in any way, I'll never forgive myself for allowing her to go in without me. I understand the logic behind staying behind, but that doesn't make me feel any better about it, especially after Lily's death.

As the figures get closer, Persephone is leading the way. I rush toward her, wrapping her in my arms. After losing her friend, I can't imagine how she is feeling right now. She cries softly with her face against my chest.

"I'm so sorry, my love."

She pulls back slightly, "You know?"

I nod slowly, "Yes...I escorted her into the next life."

This makes her and Rose sob at the loss.

"I'm so sorry," I hear a stranger say.

Glancing toward the final person to emerge from the cavern, I realize that this must be Medusa in her human form, which means that not all hope is lost.

"What's next?" Rose asks, after regaining her composure.

"The Minotaur," Persephone mumbles, still in my arms.

"Minotaur?" Medusa asks.

"We have to free the Minotaur next," I explained simply.

She seems to think on my words before reaching for the golden brooch on her top. As she holds the accessory out, it appears larger than it had on her person. The golden piece is long and slender with several pieces jutting out from its base in varying lengths. The base itself is round with a set of three gems adorning it. Each gem is a different color, one red like a ruby, another green like an emerald, and the third blue like sapphire. But these gems aren't really precious stones, but rather imposters.

"What is this?" I ask, as I hand the piece to Persephone so that she can get a better look at it.

"You'll need that to get into the maze. It is the key to the entrance," Medusa says matter of factly.

"How did you come across such a thing?" Rose asks what I'm thinking.

"Before I was cursed, I was friends with Midas' daughter, princess Ariadne. After helping Theseus subdue the beast, she knew the only way to hide the fact that it still lived was to hide the key so that, no one may ever enter the maze again...including her father."

"The minotaur lives?" I can't believe what I'm hearing.

"Yes. Ariadne said that she could see humanity lying beneath the gruff exterior and couldn't bear to see it slaughtered simply because it existed. She believed that everything and everyone has a right to life." I could hear the pride and love in Medusa's voice as she spoke of her friend.

"Looks like we are headed to the island of Crete. Let's hope Midas is in the mood for visitors.

"The maze may be overgrown after all this time," Medusa cautions.

"That's not a problem." To emphasize her point, Persephone bends to place her hand on the ground. In seconds, vines shoot up to create a barrier, hiding the entrance to the cavern in the volcano.

Rose nods, and squares her shoulders. I can tell she is trying to push aside her sadness at the loss of her life-long friend.

"...what about me?" Medusa asks as if afraid of the answer.

Persephone points to the trail, "That leads to a village. You have a fresh start to live your life as you see fit." She has trouble looking Medusa in the eye, but I hear no censure or anger in her tone.

Chapter 8

ROSE

Losing Lily was the hardest moment of my life. Lily and I were born together and we lived each day together. She was my best friend, my sister, and the most selfless being I've ever known. We both knew the risks. We knew that the probability of one or both of us getting hurt or killed was high, but I assumed it would have been me, not her. My heart aches and I can't help but feel anger with both myself and with Medusa for the loss of such a wonderful soul.

I should have done something. I should have taken the lead, so that I would have been the one to push Persephone out of the way, not her. I shouldn't have let Persephone get so close to Medusa's head in the first place.

It's hard to maintain focus on the task at hand, but I know there will be time to grieve after the young princesses are found. If I remind myself of why we are here, it makes it easier to press on.

The island of Crete is home to many mythical and magical beings, one of the most famous being King Midas. Any and everything he touches turns to gold. As much of a blessing as this ability has been for Midas and his people monetarily, it is also a curse. His ability does not limit itself to nonorganic objects, so he cannot even touch his family, nor anything else that is alive.

His maze with its man-eating Minotaur used to draw in crowds by the hundreds, until his daughter Princess Ariadne helped her lover, Theseus, to best the beast. All accounts in our history archives state that he killed the beast and in turn won the princess's hand in marriage, but according to Medusa, these accounts are inaccurate.

If the Minotaur truly *is* alive in that maze, then we will be in grave danger. I know The Fates want Persephone and Hades to free him, but I can't help but feel as though we are walking into a trap.

"Where do we go from here?" I ask as we reach the base of King Midas's estate.

Hades looks around. There is a grand castle to the left, gold shining bright in the sun, and to the right is what appears to be the perimeter of the legendary maze. Gates taller than a single story home, stand firm at the entrance. It's safe to assume that they are locked, since no one has entered the maze since the beast was claimed to be killed...since the key was given to Medusa.

"We split up. Rose, I want you to go with Persephone to the castle, while I attempt to tackle that maze."

"What? No!" Persephone protests.

He grasps her by the biceps, forcing her to focus on him. "I need the two of you to create a distraction. He's not going to just allow us into his maze, especially since the key is supposed to be missing."

"It's too dangerous to go in alone," she argues.

"Both options are dangerous, my Lady. Think about it logically. Don't let your fear or emotion get in the way of our end goal. We have to do this so we can get your children back safely." I don't know who I'm trying to convince most, her or myself.

"We wouldn't even have to do all these tasks if Zeus would have left us alone!" she says frustrated.

"You are so sure that it's my brother, why?" Hades asks.

Averting her gaze, she steps away from Hades. "Let's get this over with, so we can move on to the final task."

"You keep bringing up my brother. If you truly believe he is behind it all, just tell me why. You keep dodging the question and it seems more and more like you have a vendetta against him."

I watch as her jaw drops. "You honestly think that little of me that I would hold some kind of ill will against someone for no reason?"

"That's not what I said," Hades grumbles.

I can see the anger building in both of them, and I know that can't lead to anything good. "Come on, my Lady. Let's go cause a stir and distract one king while another tries to tame the wild beast within the maze."

Hades growls in frustration, but Persephone walks ahead of me, moving swiftly toward the castle. He watches us until we are about halfway before he turns to make his way to the maze entrance.

"I don't think you two should be fighting right now, my Lady."

"I know," is all she says.

I don't know what her issue is with Zeus, but I know Persephone and I also know that she wouldn't feel that way about someone unless they gave her good reason. She is too kind as it is, even toward those who do not deserve it.

PERSEPHONE

Our argument plays out over and over in my head. Deep down, I know that I'm more angry with myself than I am with Hades. He doesn't know. No one knows about Zeus and his harassment and threats over the years. Maybe if Hades knew, we wouldn't be in this situation to begin with. *Maybe I should have told him when it all started.* Maybe this is proof that I need to finally tell him. I feel like a prisoner trapped inside my own mind.

I could feel Rose's gaze on me from behind, her eyes burrowed into the back of my skull. I'm sure she was full of unanswered questions, but she wisely keeps them to herself. Now is most definitely not the time for that kind of conversation.

"How are we going to distract the guards?" Rose asks as we make our way toward the courtyard to the left of the grand castle, using the tree line that surrounds the perimeter as cover. Taking a moment, I survey our surroundings, I can only hope that inspiration will strike.

In the courtyard, there is a fancy stable, a large ornate fountain and what looks like a blacksmith's shop. Whatever we do, it needs to draw the guards from their posts. Not just some of them, it needs to be all of them; preferably something that will also draw King Midas from within his castle.

As the wheels in my mind turn, a plan begins to form. I just hope it works.

"Rose, I need you to clear the stable. Be careful not to be seen," I instruct as my focus remains on the other building in the courtyard.

"What are you going to do, my Lady?" she asks.

"Just make sure that you get all of the horses far from the stables, check for barn cats too."

"Get the animals out. Got it."

I watch as she sneaks into the large barn-like structure. Once I'm sure that she has not been seen, I make my way toward my target. Passing the stable, I see Rose leading half a dozen horses through the rear exit toward the treeline we had been hiding in minutes before. Hastening my pace, I stop outside of the smithy's door, listening for any sign of someone inside.

There is a hissing sound that reminds me of hot metal hitting cold water. As the hissing sound slows, I crack the door open enough to see inside. The blacksmith sets the piece he's been working on safely on his work bench. Wiping his brow, he removes his heat protective gloves and takes a drink from a large flask.

I watch as he tinkers with something on a counter beside the forge, then walks toward the back of the shop and disappears behind a door. Could he be on break? Unsure of how much time I have, I take a deep breath before entering the shop. When this plan came to mind, I didn't think through the logistics of it. As I look around, I decide my best option is to use the gloves I saw the blacksmith remove.

Once I've put the thick material on, I find a thick bucket made of a metal I am not familiar with. It looks charred but there are no melted spots.

Please let this work, I think to myself as I use one of the metal rods made for stoking the fire. Placing the bucket as close to the mouth of the forge as I can, I use the rod to pull several of the hot coals out. Once I've filled the bucket with flaming coals, I rush to the door. Even through the thick protective gloves, I can feel the heat building.

I peek my head out to make sure the coast is clear, before continuing on to the stable. There is no sign of Rose, and I don't feel any life forces within, which means no one will be hurt by the fire I plan to start. If I want this plan to work, I'm going to need the fire to spread quickly.

There are six stalls, three on each side, and one large surplus of dry hay in the back. I spread small bits of hot coal in each stall before putting the rest at the base of the mountain of hay bales in the back. The flames ignite the hay almost immediately. As the smoke begins to build, I rush out the rear exit toward where I saw Rose taking the horses.

Behind me, I hear shouting and the sound of feet moving quickly against stone. I don't turn to see my handiwork until I'm safely hidden within the trees. Rose is staring behind me, slack jawed and eyes wide. As I turn to see the destruction for myself, I'm surprised to see a wall of thick black smoke. Orange and red flames flicker within the wall of smoke. Guards and other castle staff run around with buckets of water, desperately trying to extinguish the flames.

"Effective," Rose says, unable to look away.

I grab her arm, pulling her attention away from the commotion. "Come on, we need to make sure Hades doesn't need our help."

As soon as I say the words, I get an awful feeling in my gut, a feeling of intense dread.

At the entrance of the maze, I know that finding our way through will take forever. I can feel Hades' life force deep within. Using his location as a beacon, I call the nearby roots forth. I watch the roots weave themselves together as they stretch further and further. It takes a great deal of effort and concentration, but I manage to create a low bridge through the maze to the location I felt Hades' life force.

He should be able to see the bridge and use it to escape the maze.

The longer time passes, the more concerned I become.

"My Lady, shouldn't he have come out by now?" Rose voices the question I've been too afraid to ask.

That feeling in my gut has intensified.

"Should we-" But Rose doesn't get to finish her questions. I'm already walking on the bridge I've made, into the maze.

HADES

There is no doubt in my mind that there is more to Persephone's feelings toward my brother, I just don't know what that is. It frustrates me to no end that she doesn't trust me enough to tell me what it is. I've never given her any reason to doubt me, or to think she can't trust me. Whatever it is, it must be bad for her to think he is capable of kidnapping his own nieces.

Rose is right, we need to focus on our tasks and not our argument. Shaking my head, I try to focus on stealth. If I can make it to the entrance unseen, I'll have a better chance of gaining access before anyone can stop me. Once inside, it won't be difficult for me to ascertain the Minotaur's location. It is a living being and as such has a soul. As the god of death, I'll be able to locate its soul and use that as a beacon to follow.

The gate is tall and sturdy. It takes me several minutes to locate the keyhole because of the overgrowth of vines from the maze sides. Pulling out the oddly shaped key, I insert it into the keyhole as far as it will go, then turn. The locking mechanism makes a clicking sound before giving way. As I push the door open enough for me to slip through, the giant golden door groans loudly.

Looking back toward the castle, I can only hope that Persephone and Rose are okay. I close the door behind me so that it appears untouched from the outside and then focus on finding the Minotaur. The trick to most mazes is to keep your hand on the right wall and continue to walk until you reach the exit, but this maze is different. It's not the exit I'm looking for, I'm looking for the creature that lives within.

To my surprise, there are several other creatures living within the maze, most of which are rodents and other small wildlife. As I focus harder, there is a faint spark of life deep within. Watching my step, I make my way at a steady pace toward the faint pull of the Minotaur's life force.

Turning the corner after about a half an hour, the ground beneath my feet gives out. Thankfully, my reflexes are faster than gravity and I manage to grab onto the overgrowth along the wall.

I pull myself back onto solid ground and look into the pit below. Several wooden spikes with sharpened points lay in wait for their next victim. Among the spikes are the remains of less fortunate souls who previously made the same mistake in direction.

Knowing I need to go in that direction, but clearly unable, I continue on until I'm able to make another turn in that direction. I may have to back track in order to find the right path.

An hour and three boobytraps later, and I come to a strange crossroads in the maze. In front of me is a large round pillar. The pillar is about as wide as I am if I stretch my arms out to the sides. Around the pillar are six paths, radiating away from it like the hands of a clock. But the most unusual thing about the pillar is that that is where I sense the Minotaur. His life force seems to be resonating from this point.

In all the stories I've heard of Midas' maze, there has never been mention of a pillar such as this. *Could this be how Theseus hid the fact that he did not kill the beast?*

Stepping carefully around the pillar, I search for anything out of the ordinary.

On the third time around, I see three small round spaces at the base. What caught my eye is the fact that one is red, one is green and the third is blue, just like the gems on the handle of the key. Pulling the key out of my pocket, I try to get the gems out. When they don't budge, I use my flame to melt the metal of the key itself. As the flame returns into my hand, the three small gems sit in my palm.

I place each gem in its corresponding space.

As the third gem is placed, the ground begins to rumble. Dust falls around the pillar as cracks form in the large fixture. I shield my eyes as the rubble falls away.

Once the dust has cleared, I open my eyes to see what remains.

Before I know what's happening, the Minotaur's skull and horns collide with my abdomen and I'm sent flying backwards. Gasping for breath, I realize I have two puncture wounds, one on either side of my stomach from where his horns penetrated my flesh. He charges toward me once more, this time reaching forward and grasping my throat in its hooves. If he had had the hands of a man, I'm sure he'd be strangling me, but as the hooves cannot grab my throat properly, I manage to slip out from under him.

Twisting around, I quickly get out of range, but circle him.

"I'm here to help you, you big idiot." Ok, so maybe I didn't need to call him an idiot, but pain shortens my temper.

He growls but does not advance.

"Thank you would be nice, but since you seem to be more beast than human, I'll let your lack of manners slide this time." I don't expect to receive a response.

The Minotaur stamps his foot as if readying to charge.

"Seriously? I just freed you from that damn pillar!" I yell as if he can understand me. *Why did The Fates want this thing freed anyway?*

As predicted, the Minotaur charges, but at the last moment, he veers to the left and disappears within the maze.

I exhale in relief. I've lost a lot of blood from the wounds he inflicted, I don't think I could handle more of a fight at least not without killing him and that would defeat the entire purpose.

Slowly lowering myself to the ground, I take several calming breaths as I prepare myself to seal the wounds. I have to stop the bleeding so I can continue on to the next task. I'm no good to anyone like this. Calling my flame to my right hand, I use the flame to cauterize first the wound on the left. Unable to stop myself, I yell out in pain.

The smell of burning flesh assails my nostrils, but I know I'm not done yet. Switching hands, I watch the flame dance in my palm as I work up the nerve to sear my flesh for a second time. I trick myself into thinking the second one won't be as bad, after all there is only so much pain that the brain can process at once.

It's a lie. The second one is just as bad as the first, if not worse, as it compounds the agony. As my flame disappears back into my hand, I collapse. My body is covered in sweat from the pain and exertion. *I just need a minute.*

My head falls to the side and I see a strange round stone in the center of where the pillar had been. Pulling myself toward it, I wince as the rubble rubs against my wounds. But my effort is rewarded as I focus on the round stone and realize that it is an ancient map leading to the one place we need to go next. It's all starting to make sense now. We needed to get the key from Medusa in order to get into the maze. We needed to get into the maze in order to free the Minotaur so that we could get the map to the cave where Amalthea used to live. The horn must be there.

With the momentary relief at finding the true reasons for all these tasks, my body gives out. My strength will regenerate soon, but for now, I need to rest. Even gods need time to heal.

***

"Hades! Hades, wake up." Persephone's voice cuts through the haze bringing me back to consciousness.

"Wh-" I jump up, or at least I try to. The pain in my sides makes it impossible for me to move properly, so I end up stumbling backward.

"You're hurt," Persephone says as she helps stabilize me on my feet.

"I'm fine," I grumble, pushing away from her. I don't need to appear weak right now. She needs to know that she can count on me to complete these tasks and find our daughters.

Looking around, I realize that there is a new feature to the maze, or rather *through* the maze.

Vines and roots have woven together to create a bridge of sorts. It has created a straight shot from where we are in the center of the maze to the entrance, or rather exit as it were.

"You did this?" I ask.

"I had a feeling...I knew I needed to get to you fast." She averts her gaze, but I can tell she is looking at all the blood on the ground.

Reaching down, I try to lift the stone map, but it pulls on my wounds, causing me to hiss in pain.

"Here, let me," Persephone says as she takes it from me. "What is this?"

"It's a map to help us find the horn of Amalthea."

Rose, who's been quiet this whole time laughs, "I guess there is a point to all of this." She sounds almost relieved, as if she had begun to lose hope.

"Let's get out of this maze. The Minotaur is loose and there is no telling what he will do."

"I don't understand why The Fates would want him kept alive. They have to know that his hunger for human flesh isn't going to go away simply because he is free," Persephone says.

"My guess is he has a role of his own to play in the world," Rose says, but we all look around to make sure the Minotaur isn't watching us.

Our pace is slow but steady as we walk along the bridge Persephone has created for us. What took hours initially, now takes a fraction of the time. As we reach the opening, I notice that the gate has been mangled beyond repair by the strength of the roots crushing power.

Rose runs ahead of us into the clearing between the castle and the maze, spinning around and dancing excitedly. "We did it!" she cheers.

Something doesn't feel right. My senses go on high alert as the hair on the back of my neck stands up. I survey the area, but nothing seems amiss.

Without warning, Midas appears from behind one of the lawn statues.

"Rose, run!'" I yell, but it's too late.

"You destroyed my stable. You will pay!" Anger burns in his eyes as his hand brushes her shoulder. He barely touched her, but it's all that's needed. One moment Rose is dancing in the sun, celebrating our success, and the next she is a solid gold statue.

"NO!" Persephone screams.

I reach out, grabbing her around the waist to prevent her from going near Midas.

"Why?" she sobs, as I hold onto her.

The pain from my wounds is excruciating, but it doesn't matter. I will do anything to keep her from suffering the same fate as Rose.

"I'm so sorry, my love. I'm so sorry," I repeat, hoping she hears me and can feel my love for her. She has had to face far too much loss, I won't let her think that she is alone.

All the noise must have attracted the Minotaur because I hear his hoof falls approaching fast from behind us. In an effort to avoid the creature, I pull Persephone toward the external wall of the maze. If the beast is looking for freedom, hopefully he will ignore us if we are so close to the thing he is escaping from.

I watch in amazement as the Minotaur runs straight for its master. Midas is so shocked by the sight that he doesn't move. For the king, that is one mistake he won't be able to correct.

The Minotaur leans his head forward and collides with King Midas's abdomen, similar to how the beast had attacked me. His horns bury deep into the king's flesh, knocking him to the ground. As the beast's horns penetrate all the way through the king's body, they sink into the earth beneath King Midas.

In an attempt to stop the beast, Midas had put his hands out. Too late, his hand connected with the Minotaur's fur, turning it into solid gold. Now the king lay impaled in two places by a two-ton solid gold beast. As he coughs, blood pours from his mouth, and I know that I'll soon have another soul to escort into the afterlife.

ROSE

It happened so fast. One moment I was alive and the next? Not. It's strange. I thought it would hurt or that I'd be distraught, but I didn't feel anything. The only thing that is upsetting is the fact that I have to leave Persephone alone in this cruel world.

"I can give you a moment to say good-bye, but that is all. If we wait too long, your soul will diminish," Hades says in a soothing tone.

He walks with me to where Persephone is draped over the golden statue that was once my body. Her tears seem endless.

Nodding to Hades, he parts the veil between the world of the living and that of the dead.

"Please don't cry for me, my Lady."

She gasps before turning to see me standing next to Hades. "Oh, Rose, I'm so sorry," she cries even harder as she hugs me.

"You have nothing to be sorry for, my Lady. I lived a wonderful life, and now it's my time to move on to the next one," I try to reassure her.

"It's all my fault."

"No, never think that." I can't let her feel guilt over my death. "The only one to blame for my death is Midas, and I can see, he got what he deserved."

"I don't know what I'm going to do without you," she says between sobs.

"You are going to *live*, Persephone. You are going to find those girls, and then you are going to live a full happy life with this hunk," I say gesturing toward Hades.

She laughs, before wiping her nose in a most unladylike manner.

"I'm sorry, ladies, but we have to be going. I need to get Rose to the other side," Hades says apologetically.

"I understand," I say as I hug Persephone one last time. I begin to choke up myself as I realize that I will never see my dear friend again, but I push the emotion aside, she doesn't need to worry about me. "Okay, I'm ready."

"Lily is waiting," Hades whispers in my ear before he ushers me through the portal.

Chapter 9

PERSEPHONE

While I waited for Hades to return, I fumbled clumsily with the stone map trying to study it. My frustration was growing trying to figure out what the map was supposed to mean to us in our search to find our girls.

The map was of the island of Crete with the tri-colored jewel symbols on Mount Dikte. After everything that has happened recently, I needed some time to clear my head, so I took the map with me so that I could study it while I relaxed under a nearby tree.

Hades reappeared looking around for me, for a moment I just sat off hidden trying to catch my breath and wrap my head around the events of everything that has happened recently. Out of the corner of my eye, I can see Hades looking for me, concern written all over his face.

"Persephone?" Hades called out, *I just needed one more moment to gather myself.* "PERSEPHONE!" he yelled out in fear.

I jumped up yelling, "I'm here!" I didn't want to worry him, I just needed some time to myself.

"Why didn't you answer me? Why did you worry me, knowing the danger that we're facing?!" he said in disbelief.

"Because I needed a moment to myself! I just needed to breathe without someone needing me or watching my every move, Hades!"

"Why am I public enemy number one to you now? I am always on your side! I always have been and I always will be," he pleaded.

"You wouldn't understand half of the things I have had to endure all these years alone, Hades! Being a full-time parent, having to make all the decisions and hope that you don't make the wrong ones because you know it could alter the course of their lives! I have been carrying the load of everything!" I screeched, letting all of my frustration unload onto Hades.

"You've carried everything? How do you think I've felt all these years being forced to live on the outside looking in! Missing out on our daughters growing up, missing all of the firsts! Having to use a messenger to send and receive gifts or letters with you! I worked hard to keep you all safe from harm! Sending security to help watch over the girls when they were hidden. Then having to build a relationship with them after all that time apart, as a complete stranger when I should have been there all along. I have been struggling with just as much pain and suffering as you have!"

"Obviously there is no use trying to talk to you about this." I stormed off opening a portal as I glanced at the stone map.

I didn't bother to even look back to see if he followed me, I needed some space. Well maybe we both did, if we kept going at the pace we were we might end up saying something we would both regret.

The crunching of grass sounded behind me, making me aware of Hades' presence coming through the portal. He was silent, probably coming to the same conclusion as I have. It's safer for us to both stay silent.

His hand gripped my upper arm, forcing me to pause mid-step, "Why are we on Mount Dikte?"

When I don't respond, he pleads, "Please just talk to me!"

"The map. It appears as though the horn of Amalthea is hidden here. As far as everything else goes...we've both been hurting and it's obvious that we've been hiding it from one another. For now, I think it's best if we focus on the task at hand and worry about ourselves later. Remember what The Fates said? Time's not on our side," I said dryly, showing him the map.

We follow the map's instructions until we reach the eastern wall of the mountain. Searching the grounds on Mount Dikte, Hades found where the jewels marked a cave entrance. There was an invisible shield blocking us from entering. Hades was able to remove it easily. It was a breath of fresh air to not have anything jumping out at us.

There was an opening in the center where a statue of Amalthea stood. The horn, which had once broken off of the creature, was placed where it should be on her anatomy. This was starting to feel like a typical pattern of gods and their hidden places. Very cliche and unoriginal in my opinion for them but then again they were gods so enough said.

Hades took the horn from Amalthea's statue and examined it. "Now what?"

"I don't know." Something inside of me just cracked as I threw the stone map against the wall weeping, feeling defeated by this entire charade.

As I sunk to the ground crying, Hades was by my side catching me in his arms. "It's okay, Kore. Just let it all out."

And I did, I cried and wept until there was nothing left to give. Hades didn't say another word, he simply let me have time to process everything that had occurred.

"I'm so sorry, my love." I sat up and looked at him apologetically, "For everything. I should have never said all of those awful things to you."

"Shhh...no, my love. I'm sorry. This is no one's fault. We're both under a lot of pressure and our emotions have been through the wringer with the girls being kidnapped."

I wrapped my arms around him and buried my face in his neck, breathing in his masculine scent, letting it calm me.

Once I had finally calmed down and gathered a bit of sense back I whispered, "Why would The Fates send us after Amalthea's horn? What is so important about it?"

Hades brushed away the hair from my face, "One day, when Zeus was young and playing with Amalthea, he accidentally broke off her horn." He holds up horn as if to emphasize the point. "To make up for the pain he caused her and as a sign of gratitude to Amalthea, Zeus blessed the broken horn, so that its owner would find everything they desired. The only catch is that the horn can only be used at dawn, when the sun is just touching the horizon."

"So all we have to do is what? Make a wish at dawn?" I asked, looking the horn over in my hands.

Hades took the horn from my hands and laid it down on the ground, before leaning me against the wall. "There is nothing that can be done until dawn. That means we have hours alone together. You and me? We need time to find our center. I'm going to remind you how much I love and cherish you."

I smiled as Hades' nose ran up and down my neck, gently kissing me and setting my soul on fire with his touches. "Oh yeah? How are you going to do that?"

Hades growled letting his tongue trace the outline of my breast as they threatened to become exposed, "Why don't I just show you instead of telling you? Let me worship your body, Queen Persephone."

My breathing was becoming labored the more Hades roamed across my body, "I accept your offering Hades, god of death."

HADES

In all our years of marriage, my attraction to Persephone has only grown. I love her with every part of my being, and I hate that we've been at odds with one another throughout this hardship. No more. We will work everything out and we will be open and honest with each other.

Taking my time, I kiss every inch of her, removing articles of clothing along the way to gain better access. There is no bed left in the cave for us to use but that doesn't matter. Using a combination of our clothes, I create a makeshift bed for us to lay on. Easing her onto the soft material, I take my time as I continue to kiss her all over. With her laid out beneath me, I can't help but feel incredibly lucky to have her in my life, even throughout all of the hardships we face.

Small gasps leave her lips and I know she is aroused. "Please, Hades."

"What do you need, my love?" I ask as I have many times before.

"You!"

"You have me," I whisper in her ear.

"You know what I mean. I need to feel you," she protests.

"Do I?" I tease, as my hand finds her slick center.

"Mmmm," she moans as her hips raise to meet my touch.

Two fingers enter her at a slow and methodical pace. I suck one nipple into my mouth, as I set a steady pace with my hand.

"Faster," she begs, but I don't oblige. This isn't about fast and hard. This is about reconnecting.

I can feel her release building, but I don't alter my pace, drawing out her pleasure. She moans and whimpers, rocking her hips in an attempt to find her release.

"Not yet, my love."

"Hades, I'm so close...please," she pants.

"All in good time," I say before capturing her lips for a searing kiss.

Her entire body is trembling beneath me. The sounds escaping her are purely animalistic. My own release threatens to escape simply from pleasuring my wife. I need this. I need to make her feel like she is the only thing in the world that matters...I need her to know that she *is* my world.

"Please," she pleads again. Her hand made its way down to my erection.

I groan at the contact, but pull my hips back, knowing I won't last long if she keeps doing that. She whimpers and I know she won't be able to hold it back much longer. "How close are you, my love? Are you ready for me?"

"Yes!" she screams.

I smile confidently as I remove my fingers.

Before she has a chance to protest, I position myself between her thighs and thrust into her. The moment I'm seated fully inside of her, she screams out my name, her release barreling through her. As her body tightens around me, I hold myself in place, allowing her to soak in the sensations.

Once the tension starts to ease from her body, I begin to move. Slow methodical thrusts. I continue the same pace with my cock as I had with my hand. Her eyes widen as she realizes my intentions. The sensations are maddening, but I don't increase my pace. I want to savor every moment of this. It's not long before my balls are tightening up and I know my release is imminent. My head falls forward as I desperately try to keep my release at bay.

Persephone reaches up, cupping my face between her hands, "I love you, Hades."

Closing my eyes, I soak in the feeling of her love. "I love you too, so damn much," I groan before kissing her again.

I know I won't last much longer, but I refuse to stop until she has had another release. As if sensing my own need for release, Persephone's body begins to shake with need. Unexpectedly, Persephone pushes me to the side and rolls us so that she is on top. Reaching down, she takes my hands and guides them to her breasts.

She starts out rocking her hips in the same maddeningly slow pace I had set, but as her need increases so does her pace. I raise my hips to meet hers repeatedly. Abandoning her chest, my hands find her hips, helping her to maintain her pace as her movements become desperate.

There isn't time to stop my release as it descends upon me. Thankfully, Persephone is right there with me as I call out her name. She collapses on top of me and I feel content for the first time in a long time. I hadn't realized how much my pain at not being able to be with my family on a daily basis had been affecting me until I was forced to face it.

Exhausted, Persephone falls asleep on my chest.

***

As dawn approaches, I gently shake Persephone's shoulder. "Sweetheart, it's almost dawn."

She looks around, momentarily confused, "I'm sorry, I fell asleep on you...literally." She smiles bashfully.

"Last night was perfect," I say as I kiss her on the tip of her nose.

The blush that appears is adorable.

Persephone gasps, "Oh my gosh! How could I have been so callous? You were hurt in the maze! How are you feeling?" She investigates the cauterized wounds, as if there is anything to be done now.

I laugh, "I'm fine now, my love. Your love is all I need," I wink at her.

"Come on, let's get dressed before we get distracted." My wound has already begun to heal and it won't be long until I am as good as new.

After getting dressed, we take the horn to the entrance of the cave and watch the horizon.

"Are we sure that all we have to do is make the wish?" Persephone asks, concerned.

"No, I'm honestly not sure. Was there anything else on the map?"

Going back into the cave, we intend to collect the map. Persephone walks over to where she had thrown it the night before. "No," I hear her gasp.

I walk over to see what she sees and realize that the map is broken into several pieces, some larger than others.

"I'm sorry."

Persephone is distraught at the loss of the map, but as I look closer at the broken pieces, a flash of color catches my eye. Kneeling down beside it, I pull out what appears to be a parchment with a brightly colored depiction of a sunrise on one side, and ancient writing on the other.

"What is it?" Persephone asks.

"I think this may be the answer to our questions." It has been eons since anyone has used this language, but I am familiar with it.

"What does it say?" she asks as she looks at the parchment over my shoulder.

"As the great sun returns for another day, it shall kiss the horizon in greeting. Then and only then shall your plea be heard. Take heed that your intentions be true. Destruction awaits the greed of man, while prosperity rewards the pure of heart. Hold the horn close to your heart as you speak thine desire times three."

"Could it really be that simple?" she asks.

"I don't know, but I would make sure we choose our words wisely and keep it simple. Even a simple mispronunciation could alter the meaning of our request." As I think over the wording, we walk back outside, where we can see the progress of the sky beginning to lighten. As much as I'd love to be specific and descriptive, it's been my experience that interactions with magical items need to be kept simple.

"Hades, look." Persephone points toward the horizon. "You do it," she says as she pushes the horn toward my chest.

"Are you sure?"

"Yes, you know more about magical items than I do and I'm so worried about the girls that I don't think I could say the same thing three times," she admits.

"Ok." I nod before adjusting my grip on the horn. Taking a deep breath, I repeat three times. "I wish to know the location of Melinoe and Macaria."

The horn heats up within my grasp. A glow formed where it once connected to the goat. The heat intensified until the horn shot out of my hold. Spinning in midair, the glow became blinding. We shield our eyes as the horn spins faster and faster. All of a sudden, the horn plummets to the earth, pointed side down. The glow emanates upward, and an image appears within the light.

"They are on the island of Samos," I state, before creating a portal. There is no sense in waiting around or discussing next steps. We have completed our tasks, it's time we find our girls.

Chapter 10

PERSEPHONE

The moment we stepped onto the island of Samos, I could feel the girls' life forces. They were near and they were alive.

Grabbing Hades' arm I exclaimed, "Hades, I can feel them. They're here! The horn brought us to them!"

Hades was quiet, his brow furrowed in confusion, "I...I know this place."

I was taken back, "What do you mean you know this place?"

"Not like that, my love. This is Hera's home, where she came from." He took my hand and led me towards a grand stucco home. "After she married Zeus, this was her home away from home, mostly an escape when they fought, but she used to throw luxurious parties here."

"How in all these years have I not heard about this place?" I asked.

"The last party here was long before we were wed," he answered as we wandered onto the property.

The closer we got to the house, the stronger the pull was to the girls. "Hades, they're in the house, I am certain of it."

"Then let's go find them." His tone solemn as he forced his way through the doors.

"Macaria! Melinoe!" I yelled.

"Girls! We're here! Call out if you can hear us!" Hades yelled.

Muffled groans and banging sounded, a light vibration rumbled under my feet, "They're underneath us."

"Under?" I ask in horror. Images of dirty, mildew covered dungeons come to mind.

"There is a wine cellar beneath us."

I followed Hades as he led us to the doors that led to the wine cellar. Unsure of what we are walking into, we cautiously round the corner. Hades growls at the horrifying sight we are met with. Their bodies are bound to chairs with their feet sitting in the pool of water. Hera was pacing back and forth behind them.

"Hera?" Hades and I said in shock.

Seeing Hera instead of Zeus was a shock. The whole room seemed to spin at once and my heart sank deep within my stomach. I felt like I couldn't breathe which left me incapacitated to help the girls.

"Persephone! What's wrong?" Hades yelled, pulling me through my panic attack.

Calming my breathing, my panic subsides as anger takes its place. My head snapped up and I rushed toward Hera but she was too fast for me. She ran through an open portal back to who knows where. It takes every ounce of my training with Lytta to not follow after her. Right now, the girls need me more than I need vengeance.

"Persephone! Help me, we need to be quick. Don't touch the water," Hades said frantically.

"What is that, Hades?" I ask, referring to the water at my daughters' feet.

"The pool of Tantalus, named after an insanely selfish, rich, mortal man. He could never get enough, no matter how many riches he gained. When he died he was thrown into a magical pool, full of awful agonies that Tantalus has to bear for eternity. Hecate and Lytta's own creation, they placed the old man standing in a pool of water which nearly reached his chin, and let his thirst drive him to unceasing efforts; but he could never reach the water to drink it. For whenever he stooped in his eagerness to drink, it disappeared. The pool would swallow itself up, and all there was at his feet was the dark earth. As centuries passed, we were able to use the pool of Tantalus for other punishments, tweaking it to fit our desirable level of torment." His hand hovered over the water, "I can feel its desire since it's of the underworld's magic. Its desire is to drain our girls' powers."

I started to remove the gag from Macaria's mouth as Hades removed Melinoe's. With brute strength, he broke their bindings from the chairs. Taking each one in his arms he yanked them from the pool of Tantalus.

"Momma, we were so scared!" Macaria cried out hugging me.

Melinoe's eyes darkened, her voice full of anger, "Well, it failed. Aunt Hera's plan. I can feel my powers still within me and they're charged up full of chaos."

"I'm going to kill Hera!" I yelled maliciously.

"Not if I get there first," Hades countered.

"Are you both okay? Did she hurt you in any way?" I asked concerned, trying to reign in my terror.

They both looked at each other and shook their heads no, "Why didn't it work? How do we still have our powers?" Macaria asked.

"It has to be because of Thetis' blessing. You were both born in the River Styx, blessing you with immortality. Even though you both were technically born of two gods, the river's power solidified that immortality, adding an extra layer of protection."

Our reunion was cut short when Zeus and Hera appeared in the wine cellar, Zeus ready to fight us because of whatever lie Hera had told him.

Hades and I pushed the girls behind us and a growl escaped him, whatever may come we would face it head on, as a family.

KRONOS

Under normal circumstances, I do not intervene in the day to day lives of those beneath me, but these aren't normal circumstances. The outcome of this dispute could forever change the shape of all of creation, and I can't allow that to happen. Sometimes, I have to wait and see how things play out, but not this time. This time I had to keep an eye on everything.

Of all my children, Hades is the only one I can count on. Even after he broke the rules to spend time with a mortal, he took his punishment with grace and humility. I've watched him in the following years. He has become a better father than I could ever hope to be and he treats his queen with the respect and love she deserves. I can't say the same for my other children.

This entire situation is a perfect example of how far Zeus has slipped. If he were showing his own queen the respect a wife deserves, she would have never felt the intense jealousy that pushed her over the edge. By no means does this excuse her actions. I simply acknowledge my son's role in her actions.

Appearing behind the group, with Lytta by my side, I know that I cannot allow this event to go unpunished.

"SILENCE," I bellow, getting everyone's attention.

Hades does not turn his attention away from Hera. If looks could kill, she would be ash. Lytta stands on the other side of Persephone, helping her to maintain control over her rage, and my granddaughters are huddled behind their parents.

Zeus wisely does not meet my gaze. "Hera, you have committed crimes, most atrocious. What do you have to say for yourself?"

"I hereby question the legitimacy of the twins," she states loudly, showing courage as she faces myself and a pair of angry parents. Foolhardy courage, but courage nonetheless.

"What!" Persephone shrieks. "How could you think such a thing?"

"Don't play dumb! Zeus hasn't been able to stop talking about you for years. I'm not stupid, I know he sleeps around," Hera snaps.

"Not with me!"

"Enough!" I have to stop this before it turns into a shouting match with no resolution. "Melinoe, Macaria, step forward."

The girls appear nervous. Melinoe stands a bit straighter before approaching, her sister following slightly behind her. I see great things in their future, and again I find myself feeling a sense of pride. It is not an emotion I am used to experiencing, especially not when it comes to my blood.

I hold out my hands toward them, offering one to each sister. "Questions have been raised about your lineage. Take my hand so that I may lay these rumors to rest."

As I anticipated, Macaria is the first to grasp my hand and then Melinoe. The longer I focus on my granddaughters, the more apparent it becomes that had anyone bothered to look, they would have seen the resemblance with their father. There is no mistaking it.

A hazy image appears between the girls and myself. The image reminds me of an odd projection of the knowledge within the girls' DNA. Persephone appears from within the haze, smiling. Her head is against a pillow and her hair a mess, but her happiness is clear. From above, a man's figure comes forward for a kiss before he lays beside her. The love shining in Hades' eyes as he looks into Persephone's is something that cannot be fabricated.

Hera gasps, clearly realizing what a huge mistake she has made.

"Let the record show that the goddess of life and the god of death are the biological parents of the twin goddesses Melinoe and Macaria."

I release the girls' hands and they both rush to their parents' sides. A family whole once more.

My voice deepens with anger as I return my attention to Hera and Zeus. "Hera, for the crimes of kidnapping and attempting to drain their powers, you are hereby banished from the underworld and the mortal realm. You cannot be trusted. All will hear of your actions and know the truth."

She looks horrified by my decree.

"Father please, isn't that a bit harsh?" Zeus chimes in.

"You are likewise banished from the underworld."

"What? Why me? I didn't know what she was up to," he argues.

"It is because of your actions that she was pushed to such measures. You do not think of others before you act, and you do not care who you hurt as long as you're getting your dick wet. Play with the mortals and Olympians as you wish, but you will never set foot in the underworld again."

As they begin to beg and plead for mercy, I raise my hand to silence them once more.

"I should kill you both where you stand. Thank me for my leniency and leave!"

Without another word, Zeus creates a portal that he and Hera leave through. Once the portal has closed, I return my attention to Hades and his beloved.

"Hades, bring your bride to me."

He hesitates, but approaches with Persephone at his side.

"I hereby revoke my previous decree. You have proven yourself numerous times over, and it seems you have also passed every test The Fates have created for you."

"The Fates?" Persephone asks, confused.

"Three lives. Your life with Hades is the third of these three. You will no longer be separated from one another."

"I...um, thank you...Father," Hades stumbles over his words.

It is strange to hear him refer to me as 'father' but the feeling is not unwelcome. Perhaps if things were different, if *I* were different...

"I must take my leave. Try not to cause too much trouble."

HECATE

With the girls tucked safely in bed, everyone seems to be able to take a deep breath for the first time. They may be adults officially, but they will always be cherished by those who love them, and after the experience we all had, no one wants to let them out of their sight.

I make my way into the dining room with three coffees. Handing one to Hades and another to Persephone, I take a seat across from the couple.

"I know this isn't the best time, but I have to ask," I say, directing my question to Persephone. "Do you know why Zeus would be talking to Hera about you so much?"

She visibly tenses, and I know there is something there.

Hades watches her carefully.

"I um...I don't know." She looks down into her cup, trying to ignore everything else around her.

"You can tell us, my love. Whatever it is, you can tell us," Hades presses.

Her gaze meets mine from across the table and I see tears pooling in her eyes.

"He, uh...he tried to uh...he tried to *sway* me." The way she stresses the word sway, reminds me of a conversation in the past.

"What did he do?" Hades asks, his voice full of anger.

"At first, it was all talk. He would try to flirt and when I shut him down, he'd threaten me to keep me quiet."

"At first?" I can see the anger building in Hades.

"It never stopped...He would show up wherever I was and pressure me. I managed to keep him from touching me, mostly." She laughs humorlessly, "He even tried to talk me into running away with him on our wedding day." She turns her attention to Hades specifically, "I wanted to tell you, but he had me convinced that you wouldn't believe me and that...that I wasn't worth it. I felt so disgusted with myself, it felt like no matter what I did, I couldn't stop him and over the years my confidence suffered from it...and, um...he was the one who pushed me into the well when I was a human."

Hades pulled her into his arms, "I'm so sorry that I wasn't there to protect you."

"Persephone, this is important. Did he ever..." I let the question hang in the air between us.

"No." She shakes her head, "But...he showed up once while I was bathing in the river. He took my clothes and watched me the whole time. I didn't know until I was ready to get out and he was waiting for me. He said I was a tease and that I was asking for it...He uh...he tried to corner me, but Rose came looking for me and I managed to get away."

Her tears are flowing freely now.

"I'll kill him," Hades says through his clenched jaw.

HADES

The relief I felt upon finding my daughters quickly dissipates as pure unadulterated rage fills every cell of my body. The control I've had on my anger while searching for our daughters is gone now. *How DARE they!* No one touches what is mine! No one. I feel my chest heaving with heavy breaths, and I know my eyes have darkened to solid black. It only happens when I'm on the verge of destruction, but my vision becomes more acute, allowing me more focus in my actions. A thick fog-like haze swirls around me.

Without conscious thought, a portal forms in front of me. Stepping through, I find myself at the gates of Olympus. Barriers prevent portals from forming within Olympus itself as a safety measure. No matter, I'll reach my goal one way or another.

"Hades, no!" I hear Hecate call from the other side of the portal.

With a flick of my wrist, I close the portal behind me. No one will prevent me from exacting my revenge. The haze around me swirls faster. High above Olympus, thick dark clouds form.

"Let it rain. Let the waters rise until it floods these lands," I say before approaching the gates before me. On cue, thunder cracks and lightning strikes. My brother will be distraught to find out his beloved storms no longer answer to him.

Reaching forward, I let a bolt of my own power shoot out at the barrier in front of me. The gate which was made of precious metals groans in protest as it bends and buckles under the force of my power before shattering into dust. Nothing will stand in my way.

Beneath my feet, each step I take leaves a dark patch of scorched earth. The black patches of death seep outward, as if embracing their freedom. They can seek out all of Olympus for all I care. Let it burn. At the thought, my entire body ignites in a white-hot flame. The flame is part of me, and as such it surrounds me comfortably.

The Olympians I pass along the way wisely stand at a distance as they watch the destruction death is capable of. Screams of women and children reach my ears, but I'm beyond sympathy at the moment. Several guards stand in formation in front of the home my brother and his wife share.

My eyes narrow. A few are smart and scatter, and I let them. Those who remain won't be so lucky. Placing my feet shoulder width apart, I let my flame spread onto the ground beneath me.

"What are you doing?" one of them asks.

"Olympus will burn," I say before walking past them. They can't get close to me with my shield of flame. My rage is unstoppable.

The flame rushes ahead of me, incinerating the house's entrance.

Zeus stands protectively in front of Hera, in their living room. *As if he could stop me now.*

"Hades, you have to stop this."

As the heat of my flame increases, Zeus rushes to put a barrier up between us, but it won't last long.

From the corner of my eye, I see Poseidon run in. He goes straight to Zeus' side and helps to reinforce the invisible barrier. "Hades! What in the worlds has gotten into you?"

"They will pay." My voice is unrecognizable.

I feel power stronger than anything I've ever felt before, rising within me. The house begins to groan as the structural supports melt under the heat and building pressure.

Hera slips out from behind my brothers, tears streaming down her face. "Hades, please forgive me. Zeus had nothing to do with it. It was all me, but I was wrong. I never should have taken the girls. I let my jealousy take over and I am so sorry," she pleads.

I notice Poseidon still beside Zeus and his jaw drops. Clearly he didn't get the memo yet that Hera is responsible for kidnapping my children. "What the hell, Hera!" he exclaims.

She looks at the floor, appearing to be ashamed, "I thought they were Zeus's children. He knew that Persephone was pregnant before anyone else, so I assumed she had told him. How else would he have known?" she says by way of explanation.

Poseidon's brows raise as he looks at our brother. "You didn't?"

When Zeus doesn't respond, I can't help but laugh in a humorless burst. "No, he didn't, but he tried. Numerous times, including on my *wedding day!* He harassed her so much that she felt like her own self worth was lacking. He stalked her, and watched her. Now get out of the way, Poseidon, before you get hurt."

He hesitates, before looking at Zeus, "You could get anyone, why would you hurt our brother like that? And you," he turns his attention to Hera. "Hades has been a better father to your children than Zeus ever was and he is just their uncle. How could you even for a moment entertain the idea of hurting his children, even if they weren't his biologically?" Shaking his head, Poseidon walks away from the pair.

I clear a path for him, so that he can leave without harm.

"I'm sorry!" Hera screeches hysterically.

Her words elicit no emotional response within me. These two deserve to be punished.

Raising my hands, the house turns to ash around us. Steam surrounds us as the drops of rain boil and evaporate the moment they come into contact with the flame I've created.

Before I can deliver the final blow, I'm distracted by the sound of Persephone's voice. "Hades, no!"

I hold my flame at bay, but just barely as I glare at my victims.

"Hades, this isn't you. All this destruction and death isn't you! We can make them pay some other way. We will find a suitable punishment, I promise you, but you can't let this darkness consume you."

As much as I want to listen to what she is saying, I can't soothe the fury within.

"Please don't do this. I just got my family back together. If you do this, there is no telling what the consequences might be...Never take a life before their time, remember. It's one of your most sacred rules." I feel her hand on my arm and realize that the heat doesn't affect her.

Zeus holds Hera as she cries, his eyes locked on mine as he waits for me to make my decision.

"Let me help you," I hear a second familiar voice say.

I glance to the side, to see Lytta standing next to Persephone, before glaring at Zeus once more. My anger won't allow me to be distracted for long. My body is shaking with the effort it takes to hold back.

"Let me help you, your Majesty...let me return the favor long past," she insists.

"There's no help for me, I'm too far gone," I say through clenched teeth.

"I'm going to help calm the storm inside you," Lytta says as she reaches through the flame to place her hand on my shoulder. She yells out in pain from the heat but doesn't stop.

Persephone bends down, calling upon roots and vines. They answer her call and form a dome like structure around Hera and Zeus, blocking them from my view. A second dome like structure forms around the three of us, as I feel the heat begin to cool within my veins. My vision blurs, before blinking in and out.

The flame surrounding me extinguishes, and the tension within my muscles releases. My body falls limply to the floor, as if my brain has been shut off.

LYTTA

The scent of the burnt flesh on my hand and arm, turns my stomach almost as much as the sight of it. Burnt and charred to a crisp, my arm is unrecognizable as organic material. Mercifully, the nerve endings were one of the first things to fry in the intensity of Hades' rage.

When the healers first saw the state of my arm, they pulled out all the stops in order to save the limb, but Hades' flame had been so powerful that nothing they did helped. His flame was born of such powerful hatred and rage that it became more than mere heat, it became a magical force of pure destruction. Had he allowed his flame true freedom over Olympus...there would be nothing of Olympus left. As it stands the darkened patches where his footprints lie will forever scorch the ground, a constant reminder to never underestimate the king of the underworld.

Losing the part of my arm below my elbow - hand and all- was a price I was more than willing to pay to repay a friend. I'd do it again in a heartbeat.

Had Hades succeeded in his mission, he would have never been able to undo the damage done, and he would never forgive himself for it. He may be the god of death and the king of the underworld, but that doesn't mean he is without conscience. It is part of why I choose to reside under his rule. That and what he did for me when I was barely an adult.

Years ago...a lifetime ago really. I found myself carrying out the petty tasks of gods and goddesses. I hated invoking blind rage in others, especially when it is a mere game to those ordering me to do so. After I found myself trapped with a task I could not escape, I found myself on the verge of losing control. Hera had commanded that I send Hercules into a rage unlike anything the world had ever seen. I tried to get out of it, but Hera was the queen.

Following her orders was the worst moment of my existence. I watched as his fury turned into violence...I watched as he butchered his own mortal family.

Disgusted with my own actions, I attempted to take my own life. As a goddess, it is a hard thing to manage. Hades found me instead. He offered me a place to stay, where I would never be asked to use my powers. As the years went on, I found my way in the underworld and I now use my abilities to help punish the damned.

Without Hades, I wouldn't be here today. I couldn't stand by and watch as he destroyed himself. Not after he saved me from doing just that all those years ago.

EPILOGUE

PERSEPHONE

I haven't bled in a couple of months, I paced back and forth waiting for the test to be completed. Peeing on those sticks is disgusting but I already knew the truth. After 18 years, I was with child again.

Silently, I wished for a boy. Hades needed a son. The baby fever was taking over quickly, I went from wanting this to needing this. The girls would love to have a baby brother to pick on too. Not that raising two girls wasn't fun enough but I felt ready for a different kind of challenge and one that Hades and I could share together since he had to miss out on the girls' childhoods.

The alarm went off signaling the test was complete. I stood there in awe at the two little pink lines staring back at me. I wish Lily and Rose were here to share this joyous news with and my heart ached with their loss all over again.

Before I can tell Hades, I knew what had to be done. I needed to know what The Fates knew about the new addition to our family.

THE FATES

"Ah, what a pleasant surprise," we say as Persephone enters our home.

She eyes us skeptically, "You didn't know I was coming?"

"But of course we did. It just seemed like a nice thing to say."

It is nice to see that the spark within her has not diminished despite the trials and tribulations she has endured. We may be all seeing, but what everyone fails to realize is that there are multiple outcomes based on the choices that are made.

"I struggled deciding which offering to bring," the young queen states before holding out a simple potted plant. "This is but a sprout. If you plant it at the opening of your home, it will thrive, providing you with sweet fruit to eat year round."

We study the young queen's offering. "It will do. You may speak."

"Hades and I are expecting another child. Last time...you did not have the best news for us, and if I'm being completely honest, I don't believe you were completely forthcoming. I've heard your riddles and I've passed your tests. All I'm asking is that you are completely honest with me this time."

We smile at the courage being shown. "Those who come to us seek knowledge they are not meant to know. Life is meant to be lived. It is the mystery that makes it worth living. It is important that the information we impart does not affect the fates of others."

"Is that why you talk in riddles all the time?"

"In part." Reaching into the threads, we search for the knowledge she seeks.

The thread we find is of purest white.

"Your son will take after you, my young queen. He will one day become the god of blood. While his ability may represent the life force that flows within all beings, he will choose the underworld as his domain."

"Will he be in any danger?"

We can't help but smile at her innocent yet naive question. "All living beings are in danger. Every moment is an opportunity for something to go wrong. There are no assurances in life...but we can offer you this. We see no immediate threat against your unborn child.”

Persephone appears to struggle with her words, but wisely she keeps her thoughts to herself. “Thank you,” she says, before taking her leave.

HADES

My life has been a rollercoaster for years now, changing completely from the time I was lost and confused. Adrift in an endless cycle of days and nights with no meaning to speak of, no love, no life. Now, my life is full of beautiful chaos. I have a wonderful wife who rules by my side and two energetic daughters with so much to learn still. I may have lost ten years of their childhood, but we have made up for it in spades since that time.

After their kidnapping, Persephone and I had trouble letting them out of our sight for a long time. Demeter had to talk some sense into us, explaining that if we did not give them the freedom to live their lives then they would wither and eventually suffocate. Reluctantly we allowed them to move out on their own. They check in at least once a day, and we see them regularly.

Melinoe lives here in the underworld, working directly with the dreams department, causing all kinds of drama. At least here in the underworld, my subjects watch over her and keep her safe. Macaria, on the other hand, has decided to reside in the human realm with Demeter. She will one day assist me in my tasks, helping those pass on peacefully, but for now she doesn't feel ready. It's a hard task ending someone's life, but her gift is a blessing even if she doesn't quite understand that yet.

"What are you thinking about, my love?" Persephone asks as she comes into the living room with a glass of water.

I had been sitting on the couch looking at the black screen of our television for some time now, simply reminiscing and thinking about life. I must have lost track of time. "Just thinking about life, my love." I smile.

"Oh, yeah?" she asks as she takes a seat next to me, tucking her feet up under herself so that she can sit facing me.

"I am truly blessed."

"More than you know," she says cryptically.

"What does that mean, my love?"

"I know we haven't talked about it in a long time, and we definitely haven't been trying, not that we *haven't* been trying," she rambles.

"Talked about what exactly?"

"About having more children," Persephone says hesitantly.

I reach over and pull her into my lap, "You just tell me when and where, and we'll get started," I say as I nuzzle her neck.

Her hand is on my chest, as she says, "How about nine months...or less maybe, I'm not sure exactly."

My body stills at her words. "Nine months?" I repeat, putting the pieces together. "You're pregnant?"

Leaning back, she looks into my eyes, her own alight with delight. "Yes, I still have to see the doctor to find out our due date, but I was hoping you'd come with me."

Pulling her close to me once more, I kiss her with all the hope and joy I'm feeling in this moment.

"When do we go?" I ask, referring to the appointment.

"First thing tomorrow morning."

"Good, that means we have all night to celebrate." Getting up from the couch, I carry her into the bedroom to worship her in a manner fit for a queen and the love of my life.

KRONOS

"It's been an exciting couple of decades, has it not?" my wife, Rhea says as she comes to stand next to me.

I've been spending a great deal of time at the viewing ponds of Tartarus lately. It's not that I enjoy watching the comings and goings of the other worlds, but I find myself unable to abandon Hades to the vultures of Olympus.

"Things should be calm for a while," I responded.

"It is so wonderful to see you taking an interest in one of our children," Rhea says happily.

"After the previous revolt, can you blame me?" I say, referring to the time Zeus overthrew my rule.

"No, I suppose not, but our life here is so wonderful, can't you let all that go?"

I think about her words, and realize that she is right. Without all the politics of ruling, life is much simpler.

"I'd like to get to know our granddaughters. Do you think Hades would allow it?"

"Rhea, I think he needs some time. Zeus and Hera have put him through a great deal...not to mention the punishment I issued upon him and his beloved."

"But you withdrew the restriction, that has to count for something, right?"

"Maybe. For now, let's not push our luck. From what The Fates have told me, Hades and Persephone are expecting their next child. He will be overly cautious for some time."

"I'm glad he has her. Their love is a purity I didn't think possible. Not with the way Olympus had been going." She leans her head against my shoulder as we look into the viewing ponds together.

"The love of life and death is what gives existence meaning."

My name is KAE Galla and I've loved writing since before I knew how. I'd sit with my mom and grandma telling them exactly what I wanted my story to be, and they would write it down under misshapen scribbles I tried to pass off as art work. It wasn't until years later that I finally decided to go full throttle with my passion and share it with the world. Now, thanks to the support of my loving family, great friends, and an amazing team, my dreams of becoming an author are a reality. My heart is in Paranormal Romance, and Romance in general, with "Starburst" being the first of the "A Place to Call Home" series, but I love challenging myself and broadening my horizons so you can bet there is more to come!

I'm a Native Texan, born and raised close to the heart of the great Lone Star state. I was born in January of 89' and got to grow up during a great time, I honestly don't consider myself a Millennial, and really hate that title. I Co-Own INDIE/pendent Book Services and a full-time mother/housewife, as well as a Lupus Warrior. Thanks to the encouragement of friends and family, I found a passion in writing paranormal romance books. Anything fantasy usually suits my novels and me tend to be able to reach anyone in multiple genres. Most of my story ideas come to me in the most unexpected time and places, such as my dreams. They will

plague me non-stop until I get my rear up and write it out.
Find more information about Kristen Collins at authorkristencollins.weebly.com